for Helene,
best wishes from
Stan Rabinowitz
9/90

Bethie

By the same author

Knight on Horseback

Bethie

Ann Rabinowitz

MACMILLAN PUBLISHING COMPANY
New York
COLLIER MACMILLAN PUBLISHERS
London

Macmillan Publishing Company
866 Third Avenue, New York, NY 10022
Collier Macmillan Canada, Inc.
First Edition
Printed in the United States of America

10 9 8 7 6 5 4 3 2 1

The text of this book is set in 11 point Electra.

Library of Congress Cataloging-in-Publication Data
Rabinowitz, Ann.
Bethie / by Ann Rabinowitz. — 1st ed.   p.   cm.
Summary: Growing up in New York City during World War II,
Beth's friendship with Grace is strained as Grace grows
more and more despondent following her parents' divorce.
ISBN 0-02-775661-0
[1. Friendship— Fiction. 2. Suicide—Fiction.
3. Divorce—Fiction.] I. Title.
PZ7.R1095Be   1989   [Fic]—dc19   88-22840   CIP   AC

For all children in pain,
in the hope that they may achieve insight
and the strength to survive and grow

Bethie

The December wind whipped round the corner as Beth Michaels got off the crosstown bus. As she turned north on Madison Avenue, it caught her full-face; she hunched down in her collar and slitted tearing eyes against the blast.

Late sunshine washed the buildings with rose, setting ablaze storefronts and window glass. Fleetingly she wondered whether London, now in its fourth winter of the German blitz, glowed with the same frigid fires.

She glanced up, half-fearful to spy the raptor shapes of bombers hovering. But her relief at empty skies was tinged with disappointment. She should be grateful, she told herself, that New York in 1943 was still untouched by war. Yet with an algebra test scheduled for next morning, she couldn't help hoping. Not for a citywide raid, of course. Just a direct hit on the school. Anything to stave off disaster.

In her distraction she walked right past her block. With the wind at her back she retraced her steps, scudding into Sixty-ninth Street to fetch up in front of her brownstone.

It was barely four, but the blackout curtains were already drawn. A rim of light showed under the shades on the second floor. Anticipation warmed her. Her stepmother must be having tea in the library. Beth loved afternoon tea. It was cozy. Like something in an English novel. Like a real family.

Algebra test and bombings forgotten, she charged up the front stoop. Inside, she dumped hat, scarf, and mittens on the hall table and bellowed up the stairs, "Jean?"

There was no reply.

"Jean!"

"That you, Beth?" The voice was not cordial.

"I'm coming up."

She arrived panting in the library, a narrow book-lined room that spanned the front of the house. A coal fire smoldered in the fireplace. Before it stood the mahogany butler's table set with a tea tray. The kettle was emitting its shrill whistle from the Sterno ring.

Jean hunched at her littered desk. She pointed at the tray without looking up. "Don't mind me, Beth. I've got to finish these checkbooks before dinner. Help yourself. There's toast with guava jelly. You like that."

Beth shrugged out of her coat and tossed it over the arm of the couch. Then she reached for the kettle. The handle was unexpectedly hot; she dropped it with a yelp. The pot clattered back onto the ring, slopping water into the tray.

"For heaven's sake, mind what you're doing! Do you have to be so clumsy?" Sighing with exasperation, Jean came to mop the spill. Even in anger she moved like the dancer she had been.

Beth flushed. "Sorry." She backed toward the door.

"You don't have to go."

Beth did not answer.

"Don't you want some toast and jelly at least?"

"I'm trying to lose weight," she said sullenly.

"Oh, suit yourself!" Jean snapped. "But you'd better get at your homework. Your father will be furious if you flunk math again."

Beth fled. Upstairs in her room she flopped on the bed, muttering, "Cow! Just because I dropped her old pot. What'd she want me to do—burn myself? My grades are none of her business, anyway. She's not my mother. It's between Dad and me. Besides, I'm not clumsy." This last was an old hurt. At five feet eight in her socks, Beth was taller than most of the boys in her tenth grade and towered over the petite Jean. Who made her feel a freak by comparison.

When her father had remarried four years before, Jean—with her grace, her springy brown curls, and vivid blue eyes—had seemed to Beth glamorous as a movie star. On the wedding day she had begged the privilege of buttoning the bride into her dress. That shimmering taffeta with scores of tiny buttons up the back had evoked princesses and candlelight and balls.

There was a knock at the door. "Beth, dear . . ."

She sniffed. Jean was not given to endearments, using them only when she felt guilty after one of their spats.

"Beth!"

Reluctantly she went to let her in.

Jean crossed the room to fold down on the pine child's chair under the window. Beth herself had long since outgrown it. But her mother had given it to her and she cherished it.

"Beth, I'm sorry if I picked on you. But Robert has been after me for weeks to balance the checkbooks." She sighed. "I'm not much better than you when it comes to numbers, you know. And I feel such a dunce when I make a mistake." She broke off.

Could those be tears in her eyes? Beth shifted uneasily. Tears embarrassed her. Though on her stepmother, she had to admit, they were appealing. While when she cried—which was almost never except at movies—she looked for all the world like an overgrown red-eyed rabbit.

She changed the subject. "Dave home yet?"

Jean fumbled for a handkerchief and blew her nose. "Not unless he came in through the basement and I didn't hear him. But he's never back so early." She shook her head. "No one would take the two of you for siblings. You're so different. Coloring and temperament and—"

Beth grinned a little maliciously. "You wouldn't even know we went to the same school. I'm always early, and he never gets there before the late bell. And I have my homework in on time. I'm surprised they don't kick him out."

"It's not likely," Jean told her. "After all, he graduates and goes into the army this spring." She glanced at her watch and exclaimed in dismay, "Almost five! And the accounts not done and dinner not even started. Robert will have a fit!"

Beth took pity on her. "I'll get things going in the kitchen. What's for supper?"

"A casserole. Put it in the oven at three fifty."

"One of your goulashes?" Beth said hopefully.

Jean flushed. "No. I asked Mrs. B. to leave something. I had a meeting."

"Of what?"

"Artists against Hitler." She sounded defensive.

Beth swallowed a grin. What good were a bunch of painters and dancers to the war effort? But her father and Dave teased unmercifully about it; she wasn't about to add to Jean's discomfort.

"Beth?"

"What?"

"Thanks for helping. And don't forget to wash up and brush your hair. No need to look as if you'd been caught out in a hurricane. Your father—"

"Who cares what he thinks?" In spite of her defiance, she stopped on the landing to steal a glance in the mirror. Greenish gray eyes stared warily back from a round face framed by a tangle of blond hair. She leaned forward peering. Was that a pimple on her chin? Moistening her finger with spit, she scrubbed at the offending spot. To her relief it disappeared. She ran grubby fingers through her mop and clumped downstairs.

The basement hall was still. Through the open door at one

end, she saw the kitchen lights were off. Nervous about stepping into the unlit cavern, she hesitated. Then she forced herself forward. Table and chairs were a denser black against the gloom. To her horror, a shape rose up and grabbed her.

"Gotcha!" Dave crowed.

"What on earth?" she sputtered. "Why didn't you turn the light on, you goon?"

"Been raiding the icebox. I didn't want Dad to catch me."

Her heart resumed its normal beat. She reached for the light pull; walls and appliances sprang into cold white life.

Dave pushed the forelock out of his dark eyes and grinned at her. Unappeased, she turned her back on him, struck a match, and held it to the oven. The gas caught with a small explosive pop. Spying the casserole on a back burner, she lifted the lid and peeked in. A layer of fat had solidified on top; scraps of chicken, onions, and shriveled carrot poked through the viscous surface.

"Ugh!" Dave exclaimed at her shoulder. "Did you make that?"

"Of course not. Mrs. B. left it."

"Again? You'd think Jean would. At least once in a while. What else has she got to do now she's too old to dance?"

"She's not too old," Beth protested. "She retired to take care of us."

"I don't call this taking care of us."

"Well, she has other things. Meetings and—"

"Oh, sure. Artists against Hitler." His voice dripped scorn. "I bet he'd pee in his pants for fright if he knew about them."

"You're disgusting. You sound just like Dad."

"Since when'd you join the Jean Michaels fan club?"

She slammed the casserole into the oven, announcing, "I don't know about you, but I can't just stand around. I've got homework."

As she regained her room, she heard the front door slam and

her father call out, "Jean?" in a voice he used for no one else.

Treacherous tears rose to her eyes. If only he would speak to her that way. Or even call her "Bethie." It sounded so tender. So fatherly. But Robert Michaels never used diminutives. He considered them undignified.

She gulped hard and sat down at the desk, algebra book open to the chapter on quadratic equations. Half an hour later, she slammed it shut in despair and went to the window. The street outside was dark, street lamps dimmed by wartime blackout. Houses along the block had a closed-up look, shades and curtains drawn lest convoys out at sea, where U-boats lurked, be caught against the telltale glow of the city.

She wondered what it would be like on a submarine. Dave spoke of volunteering for the navy. Beth shuddered. Bad enough on a surface ship, never knowing if or when a torpedo would slam into your side. But to cower fathoms deep as depth charges crashed about you . . . She had nightmares sometimes about being trapped in a submerged sub, water pouring through the crushed hull.

"Dinner's ready, Beth," said her father from the door. Then his face changed. "The shades are open! How many times must I remind you? Your carelessness could sink a ship!"

"I'm sorry, Dad."

"Don't tell me. Tell those sailors out there." He lunged for the shade, yanking it so hard the pull broke off. Released, the shade snapped back to flap wildly about the roller. He disentangled it, swearing, and lowered it to the sill again.

"Dad, I—"

"Forget it!" he snapped. Smoothing his thinning hair, he turned on his heel and started downstairs.

Beth trailed disconsolately after him. Once in the kitchen her spirits rose again. Jean had set a jug of Christmas greens on the table.

How could she have forgotten, Beth marveled. Christmas was almost here. Before she knew it vacation would begin. It was those darned blackout curtains. You couldn't see the decorations in windows as you passed. How she missed the festive prewar show.

She slid into her place. Her father passed a loaded plate. "That's too much," she murmured. "My diet . . ."

Dave grabbed it out of her hand. "Give it to me, then. I could eat a horse."

"After all the stuff you snitched?"

He kicked her under the table, but it was too late. Robert Michaels had heard.

"Raiding the refrigerator again?" he said. "There's a war on, you know. Meat rationing. Jean was hoping to get another meal out of that roast."

"I had gym today, Dad. It always makes me hungry."

Beth snickered, knowing the lengths to which he went to get himself excused. Again Dave's toe found her shin. She winced but held her peace.

"Glad to hear it," said Robert Michaels. "Physical fitness is important these days. You'll be glad of it in the army."

He lifted his fork to his lips. His nostrils tightened. "Another of Mrs. B.'s masterpieces, I see."

Jean looked flustered. "Well, I knew I'd be late, and I didn't want to keep you all waiting. So I asked her to fix something."

"Listen, Jean, as a cleaning woman she's barely adequate. But, for God's sake, keep her out of the kitchen before she poisons us."

"How was your day, dear?" Jean asked.

Beth cringed. She hated it when Jean tried to placate him. Not that it worked. He wasn't to be sidetracked. She supposed it was what made him a good lawyer.

For once, he proved distractable. "Hectic," he replied. "I've been asked to write an amicus curiae opinion in that civil liberties case. I spoke to Ben Abbot about it today."

"Ben?" Beth exclaimed in surprise. "Is he in New York?"

"No. I telephoned him in Philadelphia."

There was an odd note to his voice. Beth pushed her plate away. "Is Grace okay?" Grace Abbot was her best friend. Their parents had met in law school, and though the two families lived a hundred miles or so apart now, they had summered together on Cape Cod ever since Beth could remember.

Her father hesitated. "You'll have to know sometime. Ben had shocking news. Edith and he are separating."

Beth heard herself ask, "You mean getting a divorce?"

"He called it a trial separation. But it sounded pretty final to me. Edith is moving her practice and putting Grace in school here in New York."

"When are they coming? Will Grace go to Jefferson with me?"

"They're moving next weekend. At the start of the Christmas break. Grace will begin Jefferson with you after the holidays."

"What happened?"

Again he hesitated. Then he said, "Ben has fallen in love with someone else. A widow with two children of her own."

"But I thought . . ." Her voice had risen.

"What?" He did not sound as if he welcomed further questions.

She pushed her chair back and stood up.

"Where are you going?"

"To study for a test." She could have bitten her tongue. He would remember. And ask about it. He never forgot anything.

"You haven't finished your dinner," said Jean. "We have ice cream for dessert."

She shook her head and made for the stairs. She wanted to be alone. Back in her room she tried again to study. But she kept seeing Grace—face pale with shock, bewilderment in her hazel eyes, hair pushed behind the ears with that gesture she used whenever she was worried or afraid.

How could Ben do such a thing? Ben Abbot, so gentle and kind. Ben, who had come after Beth that terrible day six years before, when her father had told her he and her mother were to be divorced. Ben had not touched her, just sat beside her in the pine wood outside the Cape Cod cottage, talking quietly. Promising her parents would always be there for her and Dave. Even if they no longer loved each other. How could Ben do this to Grace?

She put the book down and went out into the hall. There was a phone extension in the linen closet. She shut the door and dialed her mother's number.

Julia Michaels answered after the first ring. She sounded unfocused, as if she spoke from far far away.

Oh, God, Beth thought. I hope she's not in one of her moods. I need her.

"Hello?" The voice was brighter.

"Mom? It's me. Beth."

"Darling! How lovely to hear from you. How's school?"

"Mom, have you heard about the Abbots?"

In the momentary pause, Beth found herself praying she already knew. She didn't want to be the one to break it to her.

Julia sighed. "Yes, Beth. I just got off the line with Edith."

"How could he do it, Mom? How could he?"

"Look, dear. You're fifteen. Almost sixteen. Old enough to realize people can't always control their feelings. These things happen."

"Well, he didn't have to fall for someone else. He's got a wife and daughter. I'm never going to speak to him again."

"How will that help Grace?"

"Grace?" Beth was taken aback.

"Yes, Grace. It's Grace you have to think of. Not getting back at Ben. How do you suppose she feels?"

"But that's just it! She adores Ben. And now he'll have another family and . . . Oh, why do things have to change? Why can't they just stay the same?"

"What about coming to see me Saturday? We'll finish the Christmas shopping, and—"

Robert Michaels cut in. "That you on the line, Beth?"

"I'm talking to Mom."

"Oh." He was silent a moment. Then, "How are you, Julia?"

"Fine, Robert. And you?"

They might have been strangers. Strangers who had never met or married or had children together.

"Overworked, as usual. Keep it short, will you? I'm expecting an important call." He hung up.

"Mom?" said Beth. "I'll come Saturday morning."

"Good. We'll go to Bloomingdale's. Afterward we'll pick out a tree and trim it."

"Neat!" Momentarily Beth forgot the Abbots and their troubles. She loved Christmas trees. Most of all she loved the magic moment when the lights were lit for the first time.

" 'Bye, dear. Try not to worry. The Abbots will survive. We did. It's a question of waiting for the pain to pass."

Beth couldn't help wondering when that was supposed to happen. Sometimes she felt she had spent the past six years waiting.

"By the way," Julia went on in a casual tone that did not fool Beth a minute, "bring Dave along. I scarcely see him these days."

"Umm," Beth mumbled. "I'll ask him." She didn't think he would agree. For some reason he avoided Julia. Hastily, before her mother could hang up, she said, "I almost forgot. I have an algebra test tomorrow. I'm petrified."

To her annoyance, Julia chuckled. "I've heard that one before. You always panic and end up getting an A."

"Not in algebra."

"Poor baby. Now, stop fretting and get a good night's sleep. I'll blow you a kiss for luck." There was a breathy sound and the line went dead.

Beth went back to her room. As she was putting her hair up for the night, her father appeared at the door.

"Beth?"

She took the bobby pins out of her mouth. "Yeah?"

"Can we talk?"

"About what?"

"The Abbots. I know how upset you must be. We all are. It opens up old wounds. But try not to judge too harshly. Grace needs your help just now. Not your indignation. The comfort of knowing someone she trusts has gone through it and come out the other side."

Have I, Beth wondered. Has any of us ever gotten over it?

"Just as your mother will help Edith," he continued. "Show her how to put her life back together."

"What do you mean, 'put her life back together'? D'you think Mom has? She still gets down in the dumps. Misses work."

A flush suffused his face. It receded, leaving hectic spots of color on the cheekbones. They gave him a feverish look. There was pain in his dark eyes, but he said evenly, "I know she still has depressions. Perhaps she always will. But there was a time when I never knew what I would find when I came home from work. Whether she might have—" He broke off. "All things considered, Julia's made a better adjustment than I dared hope."

Beth longed to reassure him. To tell him she understood. But the words would not come. She could not bear to be reminded, much less speak of those terrible days when she was small. Days when her mother hadn't gotten out of bed at all, and Dave and she had wandered through the apartment, occasionally going to her door to whisper, "Mommy? When're you going to get up?" And more urgently, "Mommy, we're hungry."

He must have read reproach in her silence, because he burst out, "I tried, Beth! God knows, I tried. When she came out of the hospital that last time, I moved heaven and earth to put things back together. For her sake. For yours and Dave's. But—"

"Let's not talk about it," she said. "I told you. I have a test tomorrow. I want to get some sleep."

He sighed. "See you at breakfast." He bent to kiss her. She turned her face aside. He hesitated an instant, then was gone. She thought he must be relieved to get back to his casebooks.

Remorse swept her. "Dad?" she called. There was no reply.

She turned off the light and climbed into bed. She heard Dave come upstairs and pause outside her door.

"You awake, Beth?"

She did not answer and presently he moved away. She closed her eyes, but thoughts buzzed in her head like hornets. She could not drive them off.

Grunting, she got out of bed again to pad barefoot down the hall to her brother's room. She found him draped across an armchair reading. He put the book down to peer at her through a haze of cigarette smoke.

"I s'ppose now you'll snitch to Dad," he jeered. "Like you did about my raiding the refrigerator. Well, go ahead. If I'm old enough to go to war, I'm old enough to smoke." He inhaled.

She waited for his coughing to subside. "I won't tell on you. Honest. It's just . . ." She could not go on.

"What's the matter?" The antagonistic stranger had vanished.

12

Once again he was the big brother she had always relied on.

"It's Grace," she quavered. "Oh, Dave . . ."

"Come sit on the bed, squirt."

She gulped. He hadn't called her that in ages.

"You're shivering. Here, put my bathrobe on." He tucked it around her. "This house is freezing! They keep it like the North Pole. I know we're supposed to save oil, but Dad's got the war on the brain."

"Oh, Dave, I thought the Abbots were the perfect family."

"It's high time you learned there's no such thing. Ben's okay, I guess. And Grace. But Edith . . ."

"She's kind of weird," Beth admitted. "But that's no reason for him to up and leave her."

"Is he supposed to put up with that zombie forever?"

"What about Grace?" she wailed. "How could he do this to her?"

"He's not doing anything to her. He's trying to make a life for himself before he gets too old. It's no different than Dad. He just couldn't take Mom's moods anymore."

"It's always our fault, isn't it?" she cried. "The woman's to blame, no matter what. You guys have nothing to do with it."

"What are you talking about?"

"Well, according to you and Dad, everything was Mom's fault. These days, it's Jean's. Like her meetings. Mrs. B.'s dinners. Now it's Edith's turn. What if she isn't so hot? Is that any reason to run out on Grace?"

"It's Edith and Grace that are moving out," he said with maddening logic. "Not Ben."

"You know what I mean!"

"For Chrissake, Beth! Don't you remember what it was like?" He stubbed the cigarette out and ran nervous fingers through his hair until it stood straight up. "When Mom was in one of her moods, I even had to change your diapers. Or you'd have stayed wet and shitty all day."

"She couldn't help it," she whispered. "Even Dad said so. She was sick."

The anger died from his face. He tried to laugh. "Hey! I was going to make you feel better, wasn't I? Anyway, don't worry about Grace. She's a good kid. She'll make it." He winked. "Gonna be a knockout, too."

She hated it when he talked that way. Grace wasn't like that. Grace was her friend.

She changed the subject. "I almost forgot. Mom wants you to come and see her this weekend. We're going Christmas shopping. And to buy a tree."

He lit another cigarette. "Get outta here, squirt. I have to finish *Hamlet* for English."

"You'll come, won't you?"

He gave her a gentle shove. "Go on, now."

"But, Dave! What'll I tell her?"

"Say I have a date."

"You don't, though, do you? Please, Dave. I think her feelings are hurt. You never go anymore."

"Tough!" Then seeing the distress on her face, he muttered, "Okay, okay. I didn't mean to get you all upset again. Maybe I'll come Saturday afternoon. To help trim the tree."

With that she had to be content. As she got back into bed, she grinned suddenly. Her math teacher always told them the best way to study for a test was not to study. In that case she was sure to get an A!

2

Snow began late Friday. By morning the flakes were falling thick and fast; the very air was opaque. The city was all but obliterated under a thick white blanket.

As Beth set off for her mother's, she squeaked in mingled shock and delight as dollops of the icy stuff slid down into her boots. Waiting for the bus, she stuck her tongue out to capture stray flakes. She loved their smooth slipperiness. In the split second before they melted, it seemed to her she tasted fragments of a falling star.

A double-decker loomed through the storm. Her excitement mounted. It was an open-topped bus. She climbed aboard, deposited her dime in the meter, and lurched up to the second level. No one else was aloft. The seats were mounded with snow. She wiped one clear with a mittened paw and sat down, pitying the passengers cooped up below.

The avenue was almost deserted as the bus sped along. Wind stung Beth's cheeks. Long before they reached Rockefeller Center, she was breathless for her first glimpse of the great Christmas tree on the mall. It did not disappoint her. Through the snow, it looked like an illustration from Grimm's fairy tales. Momentarily the city fell away; Beth was in an enchanted wood, gazing spellbound at a tree decked with a king's ransom in colored baubles.

By the Thirties, she was wet through and shivering. She got off at Twenty-second Street and headed east. As she came into the lobby of her mother's apartment house, the scent of pine assailed her. A tree stood in one corner, lavishly trimmed with ornaments and tinsel. She sighed happily. Christmas was her favorite holiday.

Grandma Michaels disapproved, she knew. "It's a Christian celebration, Robert," she would say.

"Christmas trees are pagan, not Christian," he always replied. "We're not observant Jews and the children enjoy it. So why deprive them? It's not as though we put up a crèche."

Pagan, Christian, or Jewish—Beth didn't care. Christmas was warm and bright. It made her feel welcome.

The elevator man smiled as she stepped into the car. "You're mighty wet, Miss Beth. It's a rough day out there. They say there'll be ten inches or more before it stops."

"I rode on top of an open bus," she boasted.

"That's the ticket. Fit for anything."

Julia flung the door open as if she'd been listening for her. "Don't take your coat off. We're going straight to Bloomingdale's. On a day like this we'll probably have it all to ourselves." She spoke lightly. But Beth noted the droop of her mother's mouth, the dark circles under her eyes. Her heart sank.

To cheer her, Beth said, "Dave might come this afternoon."

Her mother brightened. "Wonderful!" She got out her old beaver coat.

For Beth, the coat held bittersweet memories. During the worst of Julia's bad spells, when Beth was small, she had spent hours with her nose buried in its fur, comforted by the smell of her mother that clung to it.

As they walked up Lexington Avenue, Julia said, "Sorry to rush you out, but I wanted to leave time to pick a tree and have it delivered. I invited Tom to come help trim. With Dave here, too, it will be a real party."

"Tom Duffy?" Beth did not trouble to hide her dismay.

"I thought you'd be pleased. He's such fun. Besides, Christmas is lonely for him without his family. His ex-wife is so hostile."

Fun, Beth thought scornfully. Sure. If you happened to like dumb jokes. And drinking and smoking. Oh, Tom was friendly enough. He was almost too anxious to be liked. But she couldn't stand him. Or her mother with him. She was different when he was around. Not like her mother at all.

She forged through the snow as if trampling an enemy. She heard her mother plead, "Slow down. I can't keep up with those long legs of yours."

Beth glanced back. There was something pathetic about the small figure toiling in her wake, brown hair snow powdered as if she had aged before Beth's eyes. She waited, then linking arms, pulled her mother along. "Hurry up, Mom. There's our bus."

As they shopped, Beth struggled to recapture her earlier excitement. Try as she would, she couldn't help wishing her mother somewhere else. Anywhere but trailing her through Bloomingdale's amid a flurry of anxious queries: "D'you like this, dear?" and "What size does Dave wear?" and "Would this do for Robert?"

At this last, Beth snapped, "Why're you buying him a present? You're not married to him anymore."

Her mother drew herself up. "We're still friends. Good friends. And I'm proud of it. Other people have such ugly divorces."

Sometimes Beth wished her parents would just haul off and fight. Scream and holler instead of being so polite. So friendly. It was phony!

The sole redeeming feature of the expedition was the black-and-chrome cigarette case she found for Dave. It cost five dollars, almost one third of her budget. But she didn't care. Now he would see her for what she was. Mature. Sophisticated. Not just a tattletale kid sister. She stowed the package carefully in her shopping bag and went to find her mother.

Julia was at the handbag counter. When Beth came up, she flushed and said, "Isn't this pretty? I thought for Jean . . ." She held up a tiny satin evening purse.

Beth ached to scream, Can't you fight for yourself? She stole your husband. You're supposed to hate her! Instead, she muttered, "Oh, Mom!" and hugged her.

A trio of Salvation Army women was caroling as they came out onto the street again. Their voices wavered on the icy wind.

"Poor things!" Julia said. "They must be frozen." Dropping a coin in their basket, she joined in at the top of her lungs, "God rest ye merry gentlemen . . ."

Scarlet with embarrassment, Beth retreated. It seemed an eternity before her mother rejoined her.

"What'd you do that for?" Beth demanded. "Someone we know might have seen you!"

Her mother only laughed. They rode the bus downtown in silence. On Julia's corner they stopped to buy a tree. Beth picked the biggest she could find. "Think it will fit?"

"If it doesn't we'll cut the top off," said Julia gaily. She paid and gave the address, adding, "Be sure and get it there by two. We're having a tree-trimming party."

They were just finishing a sketchy lunch when the doorbell rang. Julia ran to answer it, calling, "Is that you, Tom?"

Beth winced at the eagerness in her voice. What on earth did she see in him?

It was the delivery boy with the Christmas tree. Set up in Julia's living room, it was even more imposing than on the street. The fragrant branches almost cut off the view from the front windows. Beth ran for the box of trimmings.

"Aren't you going to wait for the others?" her mother asked.

"They can catch up. And, anyway, Dave didn't promise. He said 'maybe' he'd get here."

Julia's stricken face stabbed her. Telling herself she didn't care, Beth tore at the tangled strings of lights. The knots seemed to have acquired a will of their own. Her mother took them from her. "Gently. You're only making it worse."

The men arrived as Beth was weaving the last string about the tree. Tom threw his arms about her and swung her off the ladder, planting a kiss full on her lips. "How's me best girl today?"

"Quit that!" she protested, wiping her mouth on her sleeve.

Unrepentant, he grinned and went to embrace Julia. "Faith and this is me lucky day. Two sweethearts in one place!"

Beth glanced at Dave. He had dropped into a chair, face averted. He would not meet her eyes.

She had to admit Tom was good-looking, she thought grudgingly, with his ruddy skin, blue eyes, and shock of silver hair. But how she hated that fake Irish charm. It might impress her mother, but it didn't fool her for a minute. Turning her back on them, she stalked into the bedroom.

Her mother called after her, "Where are you going?"

"To phone Grace. Dad won't let me make long-distance calls at home."

"Do you think you should here, then? And what about the tree?"

"Oh, do it without me!" she snapped. The taste and smell of Tom, compounded of sweat, stale cigarettes, and whiskey, still clung. Shuddering, she went into the bathroom to wash. At least the soap tasted clean.

Grace answered the phone. Relief swept Beth. What would she have said to Edith? Or Ben?

"Grace? It's me. Beth."

"Beth! Where are you?"

"In New York."

"Is something wrong?"

"Of course not. I just wondered if you were okay."

Grace gave a high-pitched giggle. "Oh, that! Silly of Popsie, don't you think?"

Beth frowned. Grace never giggled. She smiled, of course. A crooked grin that pulled up one corner of her mouth, deepening the dimples that were the bane of her life. Once in a while she let out a belly laugh. But she didn't giggle. It was odd. Unlike her.

Grace went on, "It'll be swell to go to a new school. 'Specially with you. Mummy and I are coming Friday. My vacation starts Thursday, so I won't miss anything. The furniture's being delivered Saturday. We'll be all set up for Christmas. Mummy says the apartment is beautiful. A penthouse. I can't wait to see it."

Taken aback by her enthusiasm, Beth ventured, "How about getting together Sunday? We can ride on the Fifth Avenue bus. And go to the park. It's fantastic in the snow. Maybe we'll go to the movies, too."

Grace was silent. When she spoke again, there was a pleading note to her voice. "Beth?"

"What?"

"Who comes to school programs? Like concerts and plays and parents' night?"

"What do you mean, 'Who comes'?"

"I mean, do you ask Robert and Jean? Or Julia?"

"All of them."

"Honest?"

"Sure."

"Do they talk to each other?"

"Of course! Did you think they'd make a scene?"

"Mummy would. She's always yelling at Popsie."

"She'll get over it," Beth declared with more conviction than she felt. Then she brightened. "I've got a great idea. We'll buy her a Christmas tree. So she'll feel more at home."

Grace did not seem to hear. She said, "Are there others in your—I mean, our—class, whose parents are divorced?"

"One aside from me. She lives with her mother."

"Does she ever see her father?"

"I don't think so. She doesn't talk about him."

"Oh."

It was so desolate, Beth hastened to add, "I think that's because he lives somewhere else." She remembered too late that Ben was to stay in Philadelphia.

To her relief, Julia poked her head around the door. "All done except for the star. And that's your job."

"I have to go," Beth said into the receiver. "See you next weekend."

When she came back to the living room, she gasped with delight. Her mother had turned off the lights; in the semidarkness the finished tree gleamed softly. It was trimmed entirely in blue and silver. The tinsel was so artfully placed it seemed to have drifted there. Like thistledown.

"It's beautiful! Like in a fairy tale. Was it your idea?"

Julia smiled. "No, Tom's. He's done several like it for department stores. I only hope they pay you what you're worth, Tom. They're lucky to have you."

He shrugged. "Enough to get by. Not so much my ex-wife hauls me into court for her share."

Julia frowned and said hastily, "Why don't you go try on my jewelry, Beth?"

Beth knew it pleased her mother to see her decked out in the pearls, rings, and filigree chains she had inherited from Beth's grandmother. She herself had liked nothing better when she was little. Nowadays it only embarrassed her. She felt on display, like a department store dummy. She went reluctantly back to the bedroom and returned wearing the pearls.

Julia's face fell. "Couldn't you find the rest?"

"These go better with my sweater."

"Gorgeous!" Tom exclaimed.

Dave looked up. "Hot stuff, squirt!"

If only they would shut up!

"Who wants a drink?" said Tom.

Dave rose and stalked into the kitchen. A minute later he could be heard banging ice trays in the sink to loosen the cubes.

Julia looked bewildered. "Did I do something wrong?"

Tom put a hand over hers. "It's all right, dear. Let him be."

Dave reappeared with a tray of glasses. "What'll it be?" he asked Beth.

"Ginger ale."

"How about a shot of rye in it?" her mother suggested. "Can't hurt you."

"It's disgusting. I hate it!" Her voice was shrill.

Tom laughed at her vehemence. She blushed.

Dave picked up his drink and sipped. Then he put the glass down and lit a cigarette.

"I'll put on a record," said Tom.

"Wonderful!" Julia said. "It'll be fun, won't it, Beth? We can dance." Her eyes pleaded.

Beth hunched down in her chair. Dancing made her feel awkward. Clumsy and overgrown. Besides, who was she to dance with—Tom?

As the music started, Tom pulled Julia to him. His arms curved about her. They circled the room; Julia's head drooped against his shoulder. A few strands of hair escaped their bun to cling to her flushed cheeks.

Beth tried not to watch. Against her will her eyes were drawn to them. How could her mother stand the feel of him against her?

The record ended and Tom reached for another. " 'Gaitée Parisienne,' " he announced with a flourish. "Want to see me do the cancan?" The music of the Paris cabaret filled the room. Julia's eyes sparkled. She laughed and clapped as Tom flung his legs up to the brassy beat.

He looked so comical even Beth couldn't help giggling. He should have worn lace and satin instead of a suit, she decided.

Sweat rolled down Tom's face. His breath came in gasps; his smile was fixed. "Some party, eh, Dave?" he panted. "Wouldn't your father love it?"

"Oh, yes!" Julia agreed too quickly. "You know what a wonderful dancer he is. It would be such fun to have him here. Wouldn't it, Dave?" She hesitated. "Dave?"

His face was turned away; Beth saw the red tide rise on his neck. His voice was expressionless. "I have to go, Mom. I've got a date. I'll drop Beth home on my way."

Their mother's face fell. "I thought you'd stay for supper. I ordered chicken and french fries from the delicatessen."

"Dad and Jean don't like me coming home alone after dark," Beth put in. "With the blackout and all." She stared at her mother, willing her not to cry.

Julia recovered herself. "Run along, then. Tom and I will just have to eat for four. Thanks for coming. It's been a lovely party."

No, it hasn't, Beth protested silently. It's been horrible. But it's your own fault. Why did you have to ask Tom? He spoiled it. It would have been neat without him. She scuttled into her coat and after her brother.

Once on the bus, Dave heaved a sigh of relief. "Am I glad to be outta there! She makes me feel so . . . And Tom . . ."

"I hate it when they act like that."

"Like what?"

"You know. Dancing."

To her chagrin, he laughed. "What's wrong with dancing?"

"I don't like him to hold her that way."

This time the chuckle held no amusement. "Think that's bad? Well, my puritan little sister, where do you think he'll sleep tonight?"

"What do you mean?"

"Just what I said. Where's he going to sleep?"

"At his house. Where else would he?"

"With Mom."

"But they're not married."

"So what?"

"They wouldn't. I mean, Mom wouldn't." Under his mocking stare, she faltered. "D'you think Dad knows?"

"Why should he care?"

"He's her husband."

"Not anymore, he isn't. He's married to Jean now. Why should he give a damn who Mom sleeps with?"

She thought of Ben Abbot. Suddenly he was in her mind. As clearly as if it were he, not Dave, sitting beside her.

She whispered, "Did Dad know Jean before the divorce?"

"Of course."

"Were they just friends? Or . . ." She could not bring herself to say it. She wasn't even sure what words to use.

He grinned. "What do you think? Jean's beautiful."

"So's Mom," she said loyally.

"She's nothing to write home about."

Beth winced. "But, Dave . . ."

His face softened. "Don't take it so hard. It's about time you learned the facts of life. Dad had a rough time. Mom was in the hospital a lot. Even when she was home she was always depressed."

"She couldn't help it," she choked out. She edged away from him to press her face against the window. The cold made her head ache. She closed her eyes.

She must have dozed off, because Dave had to shake her awake when they reached their stop. The blizzard had stopped but an occasional snowflake fluttered still. It seemed years since she had set out that morning.

Dave strode off without looking back.

"Dave," she called.

He turned. "Hurry up, squirt."

She stood her ground. "I felt awful leaving her like that. She had supper ready and everything. She wanted us to stay."

"I know."

"It must be lonely for her. Us living with Dad and Jean and—"

"Would you rather live with her?"

"I think about it sometimes. But when she's in one of her moods . . . Sometimes when I spend the weekend, I have to put her to bed. Or she sits up all night. And sometimes when she thinks I'm asleep, she cries."

She saw him flinch. "Shut up, squirt!"

"But other times she's fun. Much more fun than Dad. She laughs and giggles and makes silly jokes. She never yells the way he does."

"Sometimes I wish she would. She lets us get away with murder. Telling you it's okay to drink and not saying anything when I smoke."

"I guess she thinks we'll want to come if she lets us act that way. Besides, she doesn't like to get mad."

He nodded. "It scares her. I think Dad used to scare her when he was angry."

"I don't blame her. He's got an awful temper. Why do you suppose he does?"

"I dunno. He says it runs in the family."

Inspiration came to her. "I've got an idea, Dave. Let's make it a terrific Christmas for her. After all, it's your last before you go into the army. So let's spend more time with her this year. And we'll make a pact not to argue or fight or anything." Carried away, she added, "Not even with Tom. We'll even be nice to him!" She brushed away the memory of his kiss. If only it had been Laurence Olivier.

Dave squeezed her arm. "You're a good kid, Beth."

She skipped a few paces in spite of the snow. It was going to be a good Christmas. The best ever!

3

Grace's apartment house was daunting. The lobby, faced in marble and trimmed with ornate brass, seemed to Beth as big as a football field. Twin rows of potted palms conducted visitors to the bank of elevators. It reminded her of the illustration in her history book, depicting the avenue along which dead pharaohs had been borne to the tomb.

She eyed herself in the mirror, all too conscious of her shabby coat, the slush of last week's snow still staining her saddle shoes, and the triangle of torn hem that dangled from her skirt in back. She had implored Jean to fix it. Her stepmother, waspish over Robert Michaels's departure for the office on a Sunday, had snapped, "Mend it yourself. You're old enough." The words had stung. Other people's mothers fixed their clothes. But then, Jean wasn't her mother. And Julia didn't live with her.

She slunk toward the elevator under the doorman's suspicious eye.

"Who do you wish to see?"

She started. "Who, me?"

"Yes, miss. Who do you wish to see?"

"G-Grace and Edith," she stammered. "The Abbots, I mean."

"Twenty-three, miss. The penthouse."

"Penthouse," she mumbled, stepping into the elevator. The car swooped upward leaving her stomach in the lobby. By the time they reached the twenty-third floor she was queasy.

She got off and put her finger on the bell. Her heart was pounding. What was she afraid of? Grace was her best friend. What had changed?

Then it came to her. Before, Grace had been the ringleader. It was Grace who, when Jean visited Cape Cod before her marriage to Beth's father, had suggested knotting her underwear around the bedpost and planting a captured frog in her sheets. It was Grace who, when Dave and his friends lobbed firecrackers at their bike wheels on July Fourth, had grabbed them up and returned fire, sending the tormentors scampering. Now Beth would be the leader. Pathfinder through the quicksands of divorce.

The door opened. "Why, Beth," said Edith Abbot. "How nice to see you."

She could only gawk. What was she to say? Should she tell her how sorry she was? Or pretend nothing had happened?

"Come in, my dear."

She had forgotten how tall Edith was. And how thin. A gaunt, gray woman dressed all in black. Iron gray hair drawn back from a bony face. Gray eyes. Cold even when she smiled, as she did now. The eyes had an oriental look. On Grace those tilting eyes held the promise of fun. No one in her right mind would dream of calling Edith fun. When she repeated, "Come in, my dear," all Beth could think of was the wolf inviting Little Red Riding Hood in to be eaten.

"Where's Grace?"

"In her room. Waiting for you."

Beth edged past, careful not to brush against her. Since childhood she had shrunk from Edith's touch. Not that it happened often. Edith almost never touched anyone. Not even Grace. Or Ben.

A door opened at the end of the hall. Grace stood blinking as if she came from darkness into bright light.

"Oh, Beth!" she exclaimed in a high voice. "Come and see my new room." She drew Beth inside and shut the door behind her.

Beth looked curiously about. Beige walls were hung with flower prints. The furniture was unfamiliar, new and elegant. There were canopied twin beds, a bureau and desk decorated with gilt scrollwork. Two green silk chairs matched floor-length curtains drawn across the windows.

"It's dark," she complained. "Why don't you open the curtains?"

"Oh, I forgot." Grace giggled and switched on the light. Her eyes searched Beth's face. "Well?"

Beth shuffled her feet in embarrassment. The carpet was so thick her shoes sank in. She blurted out, "Everything matches." She could tell it was not the response Grace expected. She added, "No one would know you just moved in."

"We had a crew yesterday. And the new maid, Emma. You know Mummy. She can't stand mess. Like it?"

"Oh, yes! It's so—so grown-up."

Grace smiled. As if Beth had finally passed the test. "Popsie said to buy whatever we wanted. So we did. Mummy says after what he's done the least he owes us is a beautiful place."

There seemed no possible answer. Presently Beth ventured, "How's Ben?"

"Okay, I guess."

"Don't you miss him?"

"Silly! We only just left Philadelphia. How could I miss him yet? Anyway, he's coming for New Year's. To take me out."

"Where will you go?"

"He won't tell me. It's a surprise. But it'll be special. A special date. Maybe dinner and dancing at a nightclub."

Beth had never been on a date. Let alone a special one. She tried not to sound jealous. "Dad would never take me someplace like that."

Grace frowned. Beth wondered what she had said wrong.

"C'mon," Grace said abruptly. "I'll show you the rest."

She towed Beth back to the foyer, turning left into the living room. After the dimness of hall and bedroom it was painfully bright, with stark white walls and floor-to-ceiling windows across one whole side. They framed the city skyline, a forest of stone obelisks spearing the winter sky like watchtowers.

Grace pointed to the French doors. "See the terrace out there? Mummy says we'll have a garden next spring. And did you notice? The furniture here's new, too. Mummy left all the old stuff for Popsie. She said she didn't want to be reminded." The clear voice faltered. "Only . . . I just wish I could have brought my beds and things. She got to keep her Chinese rugs from before they were married." Again she paused and went on, "The dining table and chairs are Chinese, too. To match the rugs."

She sounded like a museum guide, Beth thought uneasily. Grace had never cared about furniture. She and Ben always laughed at Edith's finickiness. The way she ran a finger across the tops of furniture to test for dust. Everything in Edith's house had to be just so.

To hide her discomfort, she moved to the windows and stared out. It was as if she had never seen New York before. Gleaming in the pale sunlight, the city had a dreamlike aura. Fantastic. Like the Norman Bel Geddes "Futurama" at the 1939 World's Fair.

"Beth?" said Grace. And more sharply, "Beth!"

She started. "Sorry. I was daydreaming. Dad yells at me for it." She retreated to sprawl on the couch. The white velvet was soft, but she did not feel right. She struggled up to sit balanced on the arm.

Grace perched on the coffee table. "Well?" she prompted as before.

"Well, what?"

"What do you think of it?"

"It's beautiful."

Grace jerked her head in satisfaction. "Good! Oh, I almost forgot. You haven't seen Mummy's room."

"Couldn't it wait?"

"You have to see everything." Not waiting for an answer, she herded Beth back out into the hall and knocked on a closed door.

"Come in," Edith called.

"Are we bothering you, Mummy?"

"Of course not. Come in. Come in!" she repeated as Beth hovered.

Grace took her arm and pulled her inside. "I want to show you Mummy's bathroom."

It was like a movie set. Beth half expected to see Claudette Colbert rising from a sea of bubbles in the tub. Mirrored walls gave back her own image, mouth agape. The fixtures were blue tinted, matching towels and bath mat monogrammed and so fluffy they could have been fur. Rows of cut-glass jars and bottles lined the shelf above the sink. Beth stared. Edith never wore cosmetics, instead confronting the world with a take-me-as-I-am air that scorned artifice.

Grace tugged at her again. "Okay. Let's go."

"Go where?"

"Out. You said we'd ride a double-decker and go to the park and maybe a movie. Remember? C'n I have some money, Mummy?"

Startled, Beth swung about to find Edith just behind her. She tried to dodge past but Edith blocked the way.

"How much do movies cost in New York?" Edith demanded.

"Uh . . . it d-depends . . . " Beth stuttered. Why was it Edith always made her feel like a fool?

"You're the expert. Grace and I are just a pair of hicks come up to the big city."

Beth blushed. "Philadelphia's a city, too," she mumbled.

Grace intervened. "Don't be silly, Mummy. Give me ten dollars, and we'll get lunch out."

She said no more until they had made their escape. Then she burst out, "Am I glad to get away!"

"Well, you were the one who said I had to see everything," Beth said defensively.

"I know. I'm not blaming you. But we couldn't rush out. I'm all Mummy has now." Grace sighed. "Anyway, it's great to see you." She gave a little hop of excitement, landing smack in a pile of slush. Grimy drops spattered Beth's legs. She glared. Grace glared back. All at once they began to laugh. By the time they reached Fifth Avenue their eyes were streaming. Beth had to lean against a lamppost to catch her breath.

"Oh . . . Oh . . . " she gasped and hiccuped.

It set Grace off again. "Don't!" she moaned. "I'll wet my pants."

And with that the tension dropped away. Beth grinned with relief. It was the old Grace after all. The Grace who said whatever came to mind. No matter how outrageous.

"Oh, Grace," she cried, "I'm so glad you're here. It'll be neat going to Jefferson together. It's a wonderful school. You'll love it. I'm only sorry you missed the Christmas program."

"What was it like?"

"The whole school marched down the main staircase. It curves like the one at Tara. In *Gone With the Wind*. Remember?"

"Wasn't that a terrific movie? I saw it three times. Once with Mummy, once with a friend, and I made Grandma take me again. She said Shirley Temple was more suitable, but I insisted. I cried buckets when Melanie died."

"Me, too!" Beth sighed reminiscently. "Mom took me. I think Jean would have liked to, only she was afraid to admit she wanted to see it. Dad went on about how it was sentimental slop. You know what he's like." They both laughed. "Anyway, the school tree was set up at the foot of the stairs. We sang carols around it. The seniors carried candles and the orchestra played. Afterward we all went into the auditorium for the elementary school pageant."

"I wish I'd been there."

"You'll get to go next year. It's always the same. Even when Mom and Dad were kids and went to Jefferson. It's a school tradition."

"My school in Philadelphia was progressive. They don't believe in tradition."

"That's tough," Beth said sympathetically. "You'll love the pageant, too. The little kids are so cute!"

"What's it about?"

"Christmas. It starts with the angel. The one who told Mary she was going to have a baby."

Grace smirked. "Without you know what."

Beth hurried on. "And there's Jesus in the manger, and all the shepherds, and kings and wise men. One year I got to be a king. I wore a purple and gold robe. I was almost picked for Mary, but at the last minute they chose a sixth grader. I guess I was too fat."

"You're not fat. Just big."

"I was the first in my class to weigh a hundred. They weigh us every month in gym and call out the weights. Right out loud. Is that embarrassing! One of the boys yelled, 'Two-Ton Tessie.'"

"What did you say?"

"Nothing. I knocked him down and banged his head on the floor. He never called me that again."

Grace laughed. "I'll bet."

"There's the bus!" Beth exclaimed. She pulled Grace aboard. They clambered up and settled themselves behind the windshield.

"We don't have double-deckers in Philadelphia," Grace said.

Beth was pursuing an earlier train of thought. "Do you remember my Grandma Michaels?"

"Sure. She came to Robert and Jean's wedding. Why?"

"Well, she refused to come to the pageant the year I was a king. She didn't want me to be in it."

"Why not?"

"Because we're Jewish."

"What's that got to do with it?"

"The pageant's about Jesus, and Jews don't believe in him. At least, they don't believe he was Christ. I mean . . ." She broke off in confusion. "It's too complicated. Let's talk about something else."

Grace was not to be put off. "I don't see why Jews can't have fun at Christmas like everyone else. So what if they don't believe in Christ? Most people don't. What's that got to do with carols and pageants and presents and stuff? Why should they act different? Do they think they're so much better?" There was an edge to the words.

Beth bristled. "You know what you sound like? The Nazis. My dad says they kill people just for being Jews. He and some other men went to Washington to talk to the president about it."

"You mean he met Roosevelt?" Grace looked awed.

Beth nodded importantly. "I think so. At least they talked to someone there about getting the Jews out of Europe."

Grace touched her arm. "I didn't mean to hurt your feelings. I don't care what you are. Besides, what are we arguing about? You're Jewish and you have Christmas."

"Sure. And I love it. It's so cozy and pretty and . . . Anyway,

I don't know much about the Jewish holidays. Except for Yom Kippur. Grandma Michaels always gets cross on Yom Kippur because she can't eat. But we do. Dad thinks fasting is silly. And on Passover we go to Grandma's house for supper." She looked out and exclaimed. "That's our stop! We go into the park here to walk around the reservoir."

By the time they reached the reservoir path, Grace was shivering. "I'm cold," she complained. "Let's race." She was off without a backward glance. The ends of her scarf flashed white behind her like a rabbit's scut.

Beth pounded in pursuit, but her friend ran faster and faster. "Hey!" Beth gasped at last. "Wait up." Still Grace did not slacken the breakneck pace. Beth strained to overtake her.

Abruptly Grace stopped; Beth almost ran her down. To her horror, she saw her friend was crying. Grace cried in noisy gulps like a child, not bothering to hide the tears or wipe them away.

"You must think I'm nuts," she muttered finally.

"It's okay," Beth said. "I felt like that when my mom and dad got a divorce." The word hung between them. Ugly. Shameful.

Grace's face flamed. She wiped her nose on her sleeve. Her hand crept up to finger the charm that hung on a chain about her neck. It had been a tenth birthday present from Ben. Beth could hardly remember her without it.

"Know what I wish?" Grace said.

"What?"

"That there were no grown-ups in the world. I wish kids were born without parents. Then there wouldn't be any divorce. Or Nazis either. Or Christians and Jews. Nobody but a grown-up cares about stuff like that. C'mon. I'm getting cold again." She linked arms with Beth. They walked on.

After a time, Beth said, "There wouldn't be any school then either."

"Sure there would. Only all the teachers would be kids. You

and I could teach English. But no grammar! And we'd only assign the books we like. Like *Wuthering Heights*."

"Dave says *Wuthering Heights* is nothing but romantic hooey."

Grace tossed her head. "That just shows all he knows! I bet he never saw Laurence Olivier as Heathcliff."

"Do you remember the scene where Cathy dies and he prays for her to haunt him, so he won't be left alone in the dark where he can't find her? That was the most beautiful thing I ever saw. Do you suppose we'll fall in love like that some day?"

"I dunno. Come to think of it, Dave looks a bit like Laurence Olivier."

Beth stared. "My brother?"

"He has those burning dark eyes. And his hair's always falling into them. What does he like to read anyway?"

"*Moby Dick*," Beth replied in tones of disgust.

"Why would anyone want to read a book about a whale?"

Beth considered. "Know what I think? I think boys are different. Men, too. My father never likes the books, or plays, or movies Mom and I do. Or Jean either. He says they're just make-believe."

"What's wrong with that?"

Beth shrugged. "Life would get pretty dull without it."

"Remember the pretend games we used to play on Cape Cod when we were little? Like being lost princesses and galloping through the woods to find our castle and—"

"And remember how we used to sneak up to the attic to look through the knothole in the floor when grown-ups went to the toilet?"

"We couldn't have done that without any grown-ups."

Beth chuckled. "We could. But it wouldn't have been any fun. There's not so much to see on kids."

"We couldn't see much from up there anyhow."

"On men we did. When they stood up to pee. Ben—" Beth stopped. Presently she went on, "What'd they tell you?"

A hint of color came up in Grace's cheeks. "About what?"

"The divorce."

Grace looked away. She was silent so long Beth thought she hadn't heard. At last she replied, "Nothing."

"How did you find out, then?"

"They sent me to a psychiatrist!" Grace shouted. "They didn't have the nerve to tell me themselves."

Beth was sorry she had asked. But something drove her on. "What did he say?"

"She. It was a big fat German lady with an accent. All she said was that grown-ups have problems sometimes. That it will all work out."

"But that's not fair!" Beth exclaimed. "They should have told you. They're your parents."

Grace slanted an odd look at her. "Maybe they were scared to. Maybe they thought I couldn't take it . . . that I'd kill myself or something."

"Don't be silly!" Beth said crossly. "You have to be crazy to do something like that. They know you're not crazy."

Some of the tension went out of her friend's face. "I guess Mummy figures I've gotten used to it. She's got plenty to say these days."

"Like what?"

"Like calling Popsie a bastard."

Was it the word itself or the thought of Edith—prissy Edith— using it that shocked her, Beth wondered.

"She says he doesn't care about us anymore," Grace went on.

"That's not true. You know it isn't. Ben's the best father in the whole world. You have such a good time together. Hasn't he told you he'll always be there for you?"

"I didn't ask."

"That's what he said when my parents got divorced. About them, I mean."

Grace shrugged. "It doesn't matter. I don't care anymore. I hate him."

"But he's coming to take you out New Year's." Beth was close to tears.

"If he can buy Mummy furniture he can take me on a date, can't he? Look, I don't want to talk about it. Let's—let's talk about the world without grown-ups." Under Beth's stare, she reddened. "I'm sorry," she muttered. "I didn't mean to shock you. C'n we have lunch? I'm starved."

As they were finishing their hamburgers, Grace said, "Forget what I said back there, will you? I was just tired."

Beth had been avoiding her eyes. She slurped the last of her ice-cream soda and dared a glance. The hazel gaze was limpid. Unruffled and unrevealing.

"Want to go to the movies?"

Grace shook her head. "Mummy's all by herself. I'd better go home."

"I'll walk you."

"I can find my way." Grace slid off the stool and put a five-dollar bill on the counter. "That enough?"

"It's too much. I'll pay for mine."

"Uh-uh. My treat. Or Mummy's. She's got plenty."

Outside they faced each other in silence. Then Grace touched Beth's arm. The gesture was so swift, so unexpected, Beth thought she had imagined it.

She hesitated. "We were going to buy a tree for Edith."

"If Mummy wants one she can get it." Grace's voice was hard.

The vision of earlier Christmases with the Abbots rose before Beth's eyes. A glowing tree. Ben clowning on the ladder. Like

Tom, she thought. And immediately rejected the comparison. Ben wasn't a bit like Tom.

"Well, see you . . ."

"Have a nice Christmas," said Grace.

"I'll call you." Conscious something more was required, she added, "I'll pick you up the first day after vacation. We can go to school together."

"Sure." Grace walked away without a backward glance. At the corner she turned to wave; then she was gone.

Robert Michaels was in the hall when Beth got home. He smiled at her. "Had a good day? How was Grace?"

"Okay."

"Just okay?"

Beth did not reply. She was looking about. Funny. Most days she scarcely noticed her surroundings. While others, like today, things stood out. As if inked in with a fine point. The staircase with its scuffed strip of carpet. The hall table piled with magazines, her father's briefcase, an assortment of gloves and mittens. She felt a sudden rush of affection for them all.

Throwing her coat over the banister, she went into the living room and made for the Victorian chair shaped like a lap. Her fingers caressed the worn velvet.

"You've done that ever since you were little," her father said.

"When I was a kid I thought it was bear fur."

"How about asking Grace for New Year's Eve? Jean and I are giving a party. We told Dave he could have some friends. That goes for you, too."

"She's going out with Ben. He's coming up from Philadelphia."

"Just remember, if her plans change she's welcome here."

She glanced up, then lowered her eyes again.

"Want to talk about it?"

She tried to steady her voice. "Oh, Dad! It wasn't like the old Grace. And I didn't know what to say. I mean . . . everything I said was wrong."

"Give her time. It's still a fresh wound. And don't worry about saying the wrong thing. What matters is to be there for her." He glanced at his watch. "Look, dear, I don't want to cut this off, but I have some work to finish. Why don't you come along to the study and keep me company? We can talk when I'm done."

"Oh, yes!" she breathed. Usually only Jean was permitted in his study while he worked. "I'll bring a book."

"Good."

As they climbed the stairs, she asked, "Can we listen to Jack Benny at supper?"

"Of course."

Her heart lifted. But as she settled into the big leather chair opposite his desk, she thought, I don't understand. Ben was there for me six years ago. He knew just what to say, too. Why couldn't he do the same for Grace?

4

They had supper early New Year's Eve. Afterward Jean made sandwiches while Beth filled bowl after bowl with pretzels and potato chips. Dave and his father ferried supplies up the pantry stairs to the dining room above.

"Oh, for a house with the kitchen and dining room on the same floor," Jean sighed.

"That's all of 'em," Beth announced. "Can I make a dip?"

"Sure. What do you need?"

"Ketchup and peanut butter."

Dave grimaced.

"It's swell!" she told him. "We learned it in cooking class. Peanut butter's very nutritious."

"You'd better get used to eating what comes along," said Robert Michaels. "They don't offer a menu in the army."

"I know, I know," Dave growled. "Spam and shit on a shingle."

"Dave!" Jean exclaimed.

Beth giggled. "What's that?"

"Creamed chipped beef on toast."

Her face fell. "Is that all? We have it at least twice a week in tenth grade lunch. Don't the seniors? I never eat it. It looks like throw-up. Or creamed diarrhea."

"That's enough," her father warned.

"You started it—talking about army food." She shook the ketchup bottle vigorously. A red glob plopped into the mixing bowl.

Dave grinned at her. "Cow flop on a flat rock."

Ignoring this, she spooned a dollop of peanut butter on top and stirred. The mixture turned a muddy red brown.

"Speaking of diarrhea . . ." he began.

"I can't imagine why I send you to an expensive private school," said Robert Michaels. "Your language is deplorable."

The telephone rang. "Hello?" he said. "Oh, Grace. Do you want to speak to Beth?"

She took the receiver. "Grace?"

A quenched voice said in her ear, "You doing anything tonight?"

"No. I mean, yes. I mean, I'm not going out, but Dad and Jean are giving a party and . . . I thought Ben was coming."

"He couldn't make it."

"Why don't you ask her?" her father prompted.

"Want to come over? You can spend the night."

"I'll ask." She could hear raised voices in the background. Then Grace said, "I'll be right over."

"So he stood her up." Jean did not sound surprised.

Beth said defensively, "I guess he was too busy. Well, you know how hard he works."

The others exchanged a glance. All Jean said was, "Run along upstairs. I expect you want to change. And don't forget to put out a fresh towel for Grace."

Back in her room, she turned the radio dial to WQXR and settled onto the bed to listen to Bach's Double Violin Concerto. Presently she murmured, "Heathcliff!"

Laurence Olivier dropped to his knees beside her. "Beth. My Bethie!"

She stroked his face. His eyes burned into hers; their intensity thrilled her.

His fingers twined themselves in her hair. "Come away with me," he whispered. "I cannot live without my love. I cannot live without my life."

"Oh, Heathcliff! I would go anywhere. Do anything. Only do

not ask me to beg through ditches with you like a gypsy."

He sprang up. "You dare to fling my ancestry at me?"

She shrank before his fury. "No, Heathcliff. No! It is only that—"

There was a knock at the door.

"Blast!" said Beth.

Heathcliff vanished as suddenly as he had materialized. She swung her feet to the floor and stumped over to the door.

Grace grinned at her. "Who were you talking to?"

She flushed. "No one. I just . . . Oh, come on in."

Grace hung up her coat and put the overnight case down. "I heard you talking to someone," she insisted. "Let me guess. Laurence Olivier?"

Beth couldn't help laughing. "Heathcliff."

"Don't be a dog in the manger. Bring him back. Better still, how about Clark Gable?"

"It's New Year's. He's probably busy. But Dave asked some guys over."

"Anyone interesting?"

She considered. "There's Ray."

"Who's he?"

"Ray Siegel. Dave's best friend. He's divine."

"Light or dark?"

"Blond. With gorgeous blue eyes."

"Personally, I prefer them dark and mysterious. Like Rhett Butler. Or Dave."

"I don't usually go for blonds myself," Beth admitted. "But Ray's special. He's the only guy in Dave's class who acts as if I'm human. Not just a kid sister."

"Who else is coming?"

"Bob Davidow, I guess. But he's a creep. And Simon, of course."

Grace sighed. "Simon. My favorite name."

"Don't get your hopes up. He's got a girl."

"Just my luck! Oh, well. Maybe there'll be someone. Anyway, let's do ourselves up. The whole works. Lipstick, powder, nail polish. Then maybe they'll think we're sixteen."

"But they know we're in tenth grade."

Grace tossed her head. "It's not your age or grade that matters. It's how mature you are. Your experience. Your feelings." Beth must have looked dubious, because Grace burst out, "Oh, don't be such a stick in the mud! Look." She extracted a leather box from her suitcase and opened it to reveal a dazzling display of cosmetics.

"Wow!" Beth exclaimed. "Where'd you get it?"

"From Mummy. It's my Christmas present."

"My parents would never in a million years buy me something like that. Dad doesn't even like me to wear lipstick. He thinks I'm too young."

"Mummy says from now on we go first-class all the way," Grace told her.

"What's she mean by that?"

"Nothing but the best. This came from Bergdorf Goodman. Mummy buys all her cosmetics there."

Beth thought of the jars and bottles in Edith's bathroom. And the grayish tint to her skin. It didn't make sense. Why buy them if she wasn't going to use them?

A thought struck her. "Have you met her yet?"

"Who?"

"The woman Ben—" The look on Grace's face stopped her.

"No! And I don't care if I never do."

"You're bound to sometime. If they get married. Besides, she might turn out to be nice. Jean is."

"I never want to see Popsie again!" As she spoke, Grace's hand crept to her charm. Ben's charm. Whether from remorse or the need for reassurance, Beth could not tell. Grace let the hand drop again. Muttering, "We'd better get dressed," she took a dress from her suitcase and shook it out. It was black, with a tight bodice and full skirt cross-barred with iridescent stripes.

"That's beautiful. Is it new?" Beth failed to keep the envy from her voice.

Grace was halfway to the bathroom. "I get first dibs," she called over her shoulder. "I'm the guest."

In all the years, Beth had never thought of her as guest. But this was a new Grace. One she was not sure she liked.

"We're not supposed to use too much hot water," she cautioned. "We have to save oil for the war effort."

"Then we'll take a bath together. The way we used to when we were little."

Beth hung back.

"What's the matter? You embarrassed?"

"Oh, no. But the tub's small. Old-fashioned. Not like yours."

"Well, if you're too modest . . ." Grace managed to make it sound shameful.

Beth gave in. "I guess we can squeeze in. But there's no room to lie down. We'll have to rinse off with the hand shower."

"It's not as if we never saw each other undressed. . . ." There was a mocking gleam in Grace's eyes.

It goaded Beth. Making her hesitance seem immature. Prudish.

She started to undress. When she reached the slip, she paused, then turned her back. Stripping her underwear off, she dove into a bathrobe and belted it around her.

When she turned again, Grace was nude before the mirror. As Beth watched, she pirouetted; a secret smile tilted the corners of her mouth. Their eyes met. "Well?" said Grace.

She had been a skinny child when Beth last saw her undressed. Now in the lamplight, her friend's body had an alabaster glow. As if lit from within. Each line, each curve of the ivory form was rounded—from the neat curve of breast and belly down to where the triangle of dark hair formed a pointing arrow.

Beth blushed and tore her eyes away. I wish my hair was black like hers, she thought. 'Specially between my legs. Mine's so light you can see right through it. The crack and everything. Like a little kid.

"C'mon," she said curtly.

They sat jammed together in the tub. There was little conversation. When it came time to rinse, Grace stood and reached for the hand shower. Unselfconsciously, she spread her legs and sprayed the crotch.

Again Beth flushed. This time she could not look away. "How does it feel?" The words felt dragged from her.

"Nice. Want to try it?"

Beth grabbed a towel and fled. She stood at the closet a long time, taking deep breaths as she searched for a dress. At last she drew out the one Julia and she had bought that fall. It had struck her as sophisticated. And she had told herself the gathers would conceal her hips. But next to Grace's black, the green taffeta looked overblown. Almost tawdry.

She put on fresh underwear and eased her stockings up her legs. If only they were silk. No matter how tightly they were fastened, the rayon bagged. But silk was unobtainable since the Japanese had occupied most of China. And nylon was reserved for air force parachutes. She twisted round to straighten the seams. Then she slid the dress over her head. The taffeta rustled mysteriously.

"You look neat!" Grace said from behind her.

"Honest?"

"I wouldn't say so if I didn't mean it."

A glow rose in her. "I'll go down and see if Jean needs help. You come when you're ready."

To her astonishment, Grace clutched at her arm. "Wait! I don't want to go down by myself."

I don't get it, Beth thought. She looks so grown-up. Surprise yielded to satisfaction. If she herself was neither beautiful nor mature, at least she wasn't a scared rabbit.

The grown-up party was in full swing on the first floor. Dave and his friends had taken over the kitchen below. The strains of Harry James's golden trumpet rose from the phonograph on the table. Ray and Simon were dancing with two girls Beth had never met before. Dave and Bob watched moodily, munching on potato chips and dip.

Dave got up when the girls came in. Grace went to him. "Dave," she breathed, tilting her head to look up into his eyes.

Yuck, thought Beth.

Bob smiled and came to her. "Hi, kid. You look good tonight." There was an avid expression on his face. It made Beth uncomfortable.

She tried to capture the teasing note other girls used. "Do you really think so?"

"Wanna dance?"

She could not think of how to turn him down. He put out his arms; she moved stiffly into them. Without warning he pulled her close, squashing her cheek against his. Sweat trickled down his face. Repelled, she leaned back against his arm.

"Uh . . . H-how was your vacation?" she stammered.

"Not was. Is. We've got two more days. Remember?"

"Oh, sure. I didn't mean . . ."

She craned to see over his shoulder. Dave and Grace sat close together at the table. The party swirled about them, but they had eyes for no one else.

"How about putting on 'Star Dust'?" Beth called. "It's my favorite."

One of the girls giggled. "Your sister must be ready for bed, Dave. That's supposed to be the last song of the evening."

"I'm sick of the party, too," Bob whispered. "Let's you and me go upstairs."

She ignored him. "Anyone hungry? There are sandwiches upstairs."

"C'mon!" Bob urged in her ear. "We've got better things to do than eat."

She saw Dave pull Grace to her feet and lead her from the room. Well, why not? And if they could, so could she.

"Come on!" Bob said more insistently.

"We can go up to the library. No one's in there."

It was he who held back now. "What about your folks?"

His uncertainty steadied her. "Don't worry. They're in the living room."

"This sure is a big place. You must be rich."

She recoiled from the envy in his voice. "Oh, no! My father bought it cheap. The lady who owned it died, and . . ."

He was not listening. He hustled her out into the hall and up the stairs. His hands on her waist felt hot and intimate through the thin fabric of her dress.

She tried not to shrink. But he caught the movement. "Scared, kid? I bet you never necked. Don't worry. There's nothing to it."

They sneaked by the living room. Beth's steps lagged. On the second floor they found the library door shut. Beth would have tiptoed away, but Bob reached past her to fling it open.

Dave and Grace sat facing each other, cross-legged on the leopard rug before the hearth. The lights were off, but the firelight cast an intimate glow. Dave's face was tender.

Beth's throat closed. If only someone would look at her that way. She backed away; at that instant Grace looked up and saw her.

"Did you want something?"

Dumbly Beth shook her head. She blundered along the hall to her father and stepmother's room. The beds were piled with coats. Pushing them aside she sat down, waiting for Bob to follow. She felt neither excitement nor fear. She was numb.

Bob closed the door and stood against it. His eyes raked her. Suddenly he fumbled for the light switch; the room went dark. Beth heard him start toward her, and her heart lurched. He must have stubbed his toe because he swore. Then the bed tilted and creaked with his weight.

His arms came round her; his mouth clamped down on hers. His lips were hot and dry. They tasted faintly of toothpaste. He kept them there a long time. She began to feel sleepy; her mouth was numb with pressure. Without warning his tongue darted out—probing, predatory.

She jammed her teeth shut, protesting through them, "Hey, quit that!"

"What's the matter? You chicken?"

"No, but . . ."

He dragged her closer. His hands were on her bodice, squeezing and pinching. The taffeta squeaked under his fingers.

She fought to free herself. The door opened suddenly and the light came on again. She blinked. When she could see, she made out Ray.

"Come on, you two," he said. "The party's downstairs."

Bob let go of her so abruptly she almost toppled over. "Thanks, Ray," he said. "This was getting boring." He swaggered from the room.

Burning with humiliation, Beth tried to smooth her hair and dress.

"Don't mind him," Ray told her. "He's nothing but a blowhard. I don't know why Dave asked him. Come on. It's almost midnight."

She peeped at him from under her lashes. He was smiling. A real smile. Not as though he were making fun of her.

Dave and Grace were in the kitchen before them. Grace took Beth's hand.

"You're just in time. We're going to toast the New Year."

Dave turned on the radio. "It's midnight, everyone. Happy New Year!"

Hands fell on Beth's shoulders. Thinking it was Bob, she whirled, hot words trembling on her lips. "Happy New Year, Beth," Ray said.

Impulsively she stood on tiptoe and kissed him. "You, too, Ray."

Dave put a record on. " 'Star Dust,' " Ray said softly. "Let's dance."

They glided about the room to the sweet languor of the tune. I love him, Beth thought. I really love him. "What year is it?" she whispered.

"1944. Don't you remember?"

She went cold. Dave and Ray were to be drafted in the spring. She clutched Ray.

"What's wrong?"

"You're going into the army."

He smiled. "Don't worry. With my luck the war will be over long before I finish basic training. Besides, I'll be around awhile. They won't take me till I graduate."

"About upstairs . . ." She faltered. "I never did anything like that before. I don't even like Bob."

"That's okay. He always tries it on with pretty girls."

Happiness choked her. He thought she was pretty. She was the luckiest girl in the whole world! She had Dave. And Ray.

And her best friend, Grace, would start Jefferson with her in two days.

Her father was right, after all. She had come through. They all had. And so in time would Grace.

5

The notice on the school bulletin board read, *"Murder in the Cathedral.* All-school production. Tryouts February first. Consult your homeroom teacher for details."

Excitement coursed through Beth. February first was just one week away. And "all-school" surely meant anyone could try out. Ray would, she was sure. And so, for once, could she. Though she was no actor. Not like Ray, who was practically professional. That past year he had played leads in *Romeo and Juliet* and *Winterset.* She still choked up at the memory of those death scenes.

It was funny. She loved to cry over books and plays and movies. But when a real-life tragedy occurred—like her parents' divorce, or Julia's mother's death—she froze. At times the pressure of unshed tears felt like a balloon in her chest, choking her. But no matter how hard she tried to let go, she remained dry-eyed. At her mother's funeral, Julia had reached out to Beth for comfort. Panicky lest the dams go down and the flood swamp her, she had pulled away. She could never forget, much less forgive herself her mother's hurt.

Usually she climbed the school steps slowly, taking comfort in the knowledge that her parents' feet had once fitted themselves to the same sag in each stair. Since the divorce it had become a ritual. As if concentration on objects her parents both had touched, places they had been together might somehow mend their rift. Today she was so excited she bounded up to her third floor locker, oblivious to landmarks.

A hand touched her shoulder. She turned to find Ray smiling at her.

"D'you see the notice?" she said breathlessly. "Are you going to try out?" She stopped, embarrassed at her own eagerness. He would think she was throwing herself at him.

"Sure. Are you?"

"Uh-huh. But I'm afraid I'll fall over my feet. I'm not an actor."

"Nothing to it. Anyway, the leads are all for men. Though you can try out for the speaking chorus. The Women of Canterbury."

"Oh," she said blankly. No parts for girls? She had imagined love scenes with him. Like Heathcliff and Cathy.

Unaware that he had shattered her dream, he went on, "I'm trying out for Thomas."

"Who's he?"

"Thomas Becket. The one the play's about. He was murdered in Canterbury Cathedral."

"Was it in the *Times*?"

He laughed. "No, silly. It happened in the twelfth century. He was the archbishop of Canterbury. He got into an argument with the king about the rights of the church, and the king had him assassinated. I guess you'd call him an early resistance fighter. Like under the Nazis."

"You'll be a fantastic Thomas!" she declared. With that steady blue gaze, the stubborn set of mouth and chin, his lean strength—she could see him standing up to anyone. Even Hitler.

As they talked, she fumbled with the combination on her locker. The door sprang open suddenly, spilling the contents out onto the floor. She groaned inwardly. He would think her a slob.

The late bell jangled, startling them both. Behind her, the principal said, "Shouldn't you be in homeroom, Beth? I trust you're not planning to follow your brother's bad example."

Corraling the last of her belongings, she said through her teeth, "I'm just going, Mr. Brown."

Ray leaped into the breach. "It was my fault. We got to talking about the play. I told Beth she should try out for the chorus."

The principal looked blank. Then he smiled his distant smile. "I didn't know you sang, Beth."

She stifled a giggle. "I guess you haven't read the play. It's a speaking chorus." With that she made her escape.

Miss Gilles was at the blackboard when she came in. Beth slipped into her seat as quietly as she could. Grace smiled demurely from the next desk.

Little-Miss-Butter-Wouldn't-Melt-in-Her-Mouth, Beth thought sourly. The truth was, she was jealous. The speed with which her friend had made a place for herself at Jefferson was making Beth feel pushed out. Supplanted.

Yet the look in Grace's eyes reminded her of blacked-out windows. Allowing no light in or out. As if she could not bear for anyone—least of all herself—to know how she felt.

"Beth!" Miss Gilles said sharply.

She started. "What?"

"I said, do you have your English assignment? It's due today."

She dug through her notebook and held it out. The teacher seemed almost disappointed. "I'm delighted you're not copying your brother's bad habits. His work is often brilliant. But I've never known him to get it in on time."

Beth hung on to her temper. What was wrong with everyone? Why did they all have it in for Dave today? And what did it have to do with her?

Grace flashed a grin and flung a pellet of paper onto her desk. Inside Beth found a single word in block capitals, "Bitch!" She grinned back.

"Now," said the teacher, aligning the compositions in a precise stack, "I presume you have all seen the notice downstairs. Any questions?"

Several hands shot up. Miss Gilles pointed to Grace.

"Is there any point trying out if we haven't acted before?"

A frown drew the teacher's brows together. "There are no female parts in the play," she said. "Except for the women's chorus. And those are not traditional parts, certainly not leads. Although in Greek drama the chorus played a significant role."

"That's not fair!" Grace cried. "It said 'all-school.' Aren't girls part of this school?"

"My dear Grace, if you await fairness, I trust you are well endowed with patience. Women who seek justice must be prepared to fight. Not wait for it to be conferred as a favor. Or a right." Picking up the chalk, she scribbled on the blackboard. The stick snapped in her fingers with a sharp crack. From the rear of the room a whistle rose. The teacher swung about, eyes cold with fury. Her gaze raked the class. Then she turned back to the board.

In the ensuing hush, Beth stared at her back, thinking, Why, she's a resistance fighter, too! I bet she wouldn't be caught dead buying a present for her husband's new wife. But then, Miss Gilles wasn't married. Did she have a boyfriend? It was hard to imagine. There was nothing soft or feminine about her. Yet she was graceful. Not stiff and angular like Edith Abbot. Her face was handsome if not beautiful. And behind the severe spectacles, her dark eyes were expressive. Had she ever slept with a man?

The thought was so unexpected, so bizarre that Beth's gaze fell away in sheer embarrassment. As though the teacher might read her mind. She glanced at Grace to find her staring at Miss Gilles. The look was hard to interpret. If she hadn't known better, Beth might have called it hero worship.

Again the wolf whistle shrilled. Grace turned in her seat. "Shut up!"

Without looking back, Miss Gilles snapped, "That will do, Grace. I am quite capable of maintaining discipline unaided. Now, take out your grammars and study the next lesson while I finish putting the homework on the board."

Beth burned for her friend. She leaned over to whisper encouragement. Miss Gilles's tongue had been known to reduce students to tears. But Grace did not seem crushed. Instead she looked peaceful. As if the teacher had praised her. As if they had reached some unspoken understanding. Of what Beth was not sure.

When she got home that afternoon, the household was at sixes and sevens. The mail was still unopened on the hall table. Jean's coat was unceremoniously draped over the banister. Jean herself was in the kitchen looking harried.

"What's up?" Beth asked.

"It's that wretched Mrs. B."

"What's she done?" Beth sniffed. "Smells good in here. Not like one of her messes."

"That's just it. She quit."

"Good! I never liked her anyway. She always shoved me out of the kitchen."

Jean drew a shaky breath. "You're as bad as Robert. Always finding fault. No wonder she left. Who's to get the work done now?" She seemed on the verge of tears.

"We'll help and—"

"And there's always good old Jean. Is that it?"

"You do make good goulash. Is someone coming for dinner?"

"Your grandmother. Which means in addition to changing the beds and taking the sheets to the wash, I had to make a special trip to the bakery. You know Grandma Michaels. Without dessert it's not a proper dinner. I'd never hear the end of it if I served fruit."

Beth chuckled. "Yeah. And after three helpings of everything, she puts saccharine in her coffee and says she's dieting."

"Only she calls it 'die-eating.' It was funny the first time. But she never lets you forget."

"Why'd Mrs. B. quit?"

"She took a job at a war plant. I don't blame her. The pay's better and the hours are predictable. Plus, they get overtime. No one's ever on time for anything in this house. Especially meals. It's enough to drive anyone to drink." She sighed. "Just when I was planning to go back to work."

"Dancing?"

"Teaching dance."

"That's neat. You'll get to go out every day. Like Edith."

"Edith?" Jean sounded startled. "I don't know that I consider that a compliment."

"I suppose not," Beth agreed. "I know she's an old friend, but—"

"Who's an old friend?" her father said from the door.

"Dad! I didn't know you were home."

"Who are you two gossiping about?"

"Edith Abbot."

"Poor woman."

"Poor woman, indeed," Jean said tartly. "But she makes it hard to sympathize. You should hear the things she says about Ben. In front of Grace, too."

Her husband nodded. "I know. Incidentally, she called to ask a favor. She's leaving for Reno soon to get her divorce. She'll be gone six weeks. She wants Grace to stay with us while she's gone. Of course I said yes."

"Without consulting me?" Jean's voice had risen.

"She won't be any trouble. She's in school all day. She can share Beth's room."

"You might at least have asked. It's my home as much as yours. And I'm the one that does the work."

"You have Mrs. B."

"Not since today. She left."

"Good riddance! She never was worth what we paid her."

"It's easy for you to say. You don't have to keep this huge place clean and produce meals on ration coupons for a family that's never on time."

"I suppose that's aimed at me."

"If the shoe fits, wear it. Think of the past week."

He looked abashed. "You're right, of course. But with all the junior partners in the army . . . Sometimes I envy them. Still, someone has to practice law."

"What about all those extra meetings? Your refugee committee. Do you have to fight the whole world's battles? How about us? Aren't we entitled to some time and attention?"

"For the Jews of Europe it's a matter of life and death. They can't wait." His shoulders sagged.

Beth looked at him in surprise. It wasn't like him to be discouraged. He seemed so impervious. So armored.

Jean patted his hand. "I'm sorry, dear. I'm just crabby today. Bad as Mrs. B. was, she'll be hard to replace. And these brownstones weren't built for convenience." She turned to Beth. "Go and wash up. You can set the table for me when you come down." With an attempt at lightness, she added, "Meanwhile Robert and I will fortify ourselves for his mother with a drink."

Bursting with her news, Beth announced at dinner, "We're going to have a play at school. *Murder in the Cathedral*. It's an all-school production. I'm going to try out."

"That sounds like another of those Christian pageants," her grandmother said.

"Well, it's not. It's historical. About a twelfth-century archbishop who stood up to the king and was murdered. Right in church."

Grandma Michaels paid no attention. "Really, Robert! That school might just as well be a religious institution."

"You forget, Mother. I myself went to Jefferson. They didn't try and convert me. And it's a fine education."

She sighed. "I just wish David and Beth knew more of their Jewish heritage. You and Julia should have seen to it."

"Julia and I had other problems to deal with," he said stiffly. "And what do you want me to do about it now? Send them to some Sunday school that will stuff them full of nonsense I don't believe in? At least at Jefferson they learn about general culture."

"Sometimes I think being Jewish means nothing to you."

His lips tightened. "I spend fully half my time—unpaid—working to rescue European Jews."

She tossed her head. The war relief buttons pinned across her massive bosom flashed as she did so. Turning to Jean, she said, "This is a delicious dinner, dear. Your Mrs. B. is a treasure."

Beth put in hastily, "My friend Grace is coming to stay. Her mother's going to Reno for a divorce."

Dave looked up from his plate. "Great! We can all go to school together."

"You're not even out of bed when I leave." The prospect of Dave and Grace as allies under the same roof stung.

Jean said too casually, "I've found a studio. On Columbus Avenue and Sixty-eighth Street."

"Studio?" Her husband looked puzzled.

"Oh, Robert, you remember. I told you I was thinking of going back to teaching."

"But you've just got done complaining how much you have to do here."

Beth eyed him apprehensively. The note in his voice was often prelude to a blowup. She glanced at her stepmother.

Jean was still. Only the throbbing of the muscle at the corner of her mouth betrayed tension. "You mean waiting on all of you?"

"You make it sound like slavery. I don't call taking care of a husband and children penal servitude."

"Your children, Robert. Not mine."

Beth leaped into the fray. "I don't see why she shouldn't, Dad. We'll help. I can clean my room. And Dave—"

"You have other responsibilities. Schoolwork, for instance. And judging from that D in algebra before vacation, that's a full-time job. Besides, it's not only the cleaning. It's the meals and entertaining and . . . Is it too much to expect a little peace and comfort when I come home?"

"We'll discuss it later, Robert," Jean said. "This is neither the time nor place." She rose.

"Where are you going?"

"Upstairs to cool off. Before I say something we'll both regret. Please excuse me, Mother Michaels." She was gone before he could get another word in.

Grandma Michaels opened her mouth, then apparently thought better of it.

Beth glanced surreptitiously at her father. His lips were compressed. She hated it when he looked that way, anger threatening like a rapier. It frightened her. Remembering Miss Gilles, she screwed up her courage. "I think you were awful to discourage her. Why shouldn't she do what she wants for a change? It's better than Mom. Always giving in. Always apologizing. Doing things your way."

"My way?" His voice was deadly. "Was it my way to lie in bed all day and cry? Was it my way to leave you children unwashed, unfed? Was it my way to—"

"Robert!" Grandma Michaels cut in.

He went right on. "You should learn to stay out of things you know nothing about, Beth."

Fury overcame her caution. She squared her shoulders. "What do you mean, 'know nothing about'? I live here, too. It makes me sick the way everybody tiptoes around you. Robert this and Robert that. As if you knew everything. As if you were God! Just because you're a big lawyer and help people. You think you're so great—"

He slapped her.

For one shocked instant she stared. Then she stumbled to her feet and ran from the kitchen.

In the refuge of her room, she threw herself face down on the bed, pummeling the pillow with both fists in fruitless rage. She heard the door open; she would not look up.

"Beth?" said her father.

She burrowed further into the pillow.

She felt him sit beside her. She edged away.

"Beth, I'm sorry. If it's any consolation, Grandma Michaels raked me over the coals and Dave chewed me out. And I know Jean will be livid when she hears about this. It's my infernal Michaels temper. Please forgive me."

Some of the tension went out of her. He put his hand on her shoulder.

"I know it's no excuse, but I've had a ghastly day. Edith recited her injuries to me again when she called. And I spent hours on the phone with the State Department over the refugee situation. The reports are more and more terrible. We're trying to persuade our consulates in neutral countries to issue visas to the few refugees who still manage to make it across the borders. They keep holding them up."

Interested in spite of herself, she rolled over and sat up. "Why? Don't they want to save them?"

"They claim it's to be sure no Nazis slip into the United States posing as refugees. But actually it's because no one wants the Jews. It makes me sick! Prejudice in this day and age. People are murdered in cold blood and America sits on its hands."

"Well, it's not my fault. You didn't have to hit me."

"I deserved that," he said sadly. "By the way, I'm going to tell Jean you stood up for her. She'll appreciate it. I only wish—"

"Wish what, Dad?"

"That Jean were happier. When we married, she told me her life as a dancer was empty. That all she wanted was a home. A husband and kids to care for."

"Then why'd she say that about our not being her kids? I know she's not our real mother, but I thought she liked us."

"Oh, Beth, that was aimed at me, not you. She loves you and Dave."

"But why can't she do both? Have a family and teach?"

"I don't know," he said. "Maybe that's not the problem. I just don't seem to have the knack of keeping a wife happy."

"You're not . . ." She broke off.

"Not what?"

"Not going to get divorced again," she whispered.

He did not answer. Instead he said, "You'll help Jean, won't you? For my sake?"

"Oh, yes! I promise. I'll clean my room and do dishes and everything. Honest. I know I've said it before, but this time I really mean it."

"That's my girl." Sighing, he got to his feet. "I'd better go down to your grandmother. Or I'll be in the doghouse again."

After he had gone she went to her desk. But her hands trembled so she could not write. What was wrong with her? He had apologized. And her cheek no longer hurt where he had slapped her. But deep down she knew the answer. It was the hint of trouble between Jean and her father. The threat this marriage too might break. Once more severing the fragile web of family. She could not bear it!

She went to the linen closet and dialed her mother.

"Hello?" said Julia.

Beth steadied her voice. "Mom?"

"I was just thinking of you. Edith tells me Grace is going to stay with you while she goes to Reno."

"Umm." Try as she would, she could not sound enthusiastic.

If Julia noticed she gave no sign. "How's Grace getting along at Jefferson?"

"Okay, I guess. The kids like her. The teachers, too. Miss Gilles is always calling on her."

"Does that bother you?"

Beth was grateful she could not see her flush. "Oh, no."

"Because jealousy is human. Even between friends. You're bound to feel the competition. Don't worry. It will pass."

Only what if things did not pass, just repeated themselves? Like divorce. First her parents had been divorced. Then the Abbots separated. Now Jean and her father were fighting.

"Oh, Mom," she began. And stopped. Because this was one problem she could not share with her mother. One time she could not seek her comfort.

"What, dear?"

"Nothing. I'm trying out for a play at school."

"Will that nice friend of Dave's be in it, too?"

"Ray? He'll get the lead."

"What about Grace?"

Her heart plummeted. Until now, Grace and she had been a closed world. Now suddenly there was Grace and Dave. Grace and Beth's teachers. Grace and Beth's friends. If Grace were picked for the play, would there be Grace and Ray, too? Her knuckles cramped on the receiver.

"I have to go, Mom."

Her mother chuckled.

"What's funny?" she demanded.

"You sound like Robert. He used to call and then announce he had no time to talk. As if I had bothered him. Instead of the other way around."

She did not want to be like her father. Or Julia, for that matter. She just wanted to be herself.

"G'night," she mumbled.

"Good-night, dear. Remember what I said. A little jealousy is natural. Don't let it bother you."

She was wakeful that night. Straining to hear Jean and her father. Were they fighting again? At last in desperation she conjured up Laurence Olivier in bed beside her. Turning her head, she gazed deep into his eyes. He pulled her close. Comforted, she snuggled against his shoulder and fell asleep.

6

Tryouts were to be held in the gymnasium. It was a stormy day; sleet spattered the high windows. The cavernous space was gloomy.

Beth arrived to find Ray lounging against a vaulting horse. He waved. Heart beating fast, she went to join him. "How come the tryouts aren't in the auditorium?" she demanded.

"The stage is too small. This play has a big cast."

"It's so bare in here."

"We'll hang backdrops from the balcony. You'll see. It'll look like a cathedral."

Beth gazed about her, trying to picture the familiar room transformed into an arena for mystery and drama. It was hard to imagine. The gym was the gym. The place where they played dodgeball and prisoner's base and basketball. Recently the gym teachers had added military drill as Jefferson's contribution to the war effort. Thinking of that organized confusion, she stifled a giggle.

"Where's Grace?" Miss Gilles called from the doorway. "Isn't she going to try out?"

"How should I know?" she said resentfully.

"Don't be impertinent."

Beth reddened. Ray touched her hand. "Don't mind her."

"What does she care if Grace tries out or not?"

"I guess she likes her. I know Dave does. He can't stop talking about her."

She changed the subject. "Will Miss Gilles be the director?"

"No. She's going to coach the choral speaking. You know

how fussy she is about how we talk. Come to think of it, maybe that's why she's so hipped on Grace. It's that Main Line accent."

They fell silent, watching the other students drift in. Grace appeared at the last minute, flushed and panting.

"Where were you?" said Beth. "Miss Gilles asked if you were coming. She got furious when I said I didn't know."

"I ran into Dave. We went out for a soda."

"Did you forget the tryouts?"

"I knew they wouldn't start on time."

Beth could not trust herself to speak. Grace had touched a raw nerve. Beth was early everywhere, anxious lest others take her place.

"Good luck," she said through her teeth.

"Won't it be fun?" said Grace. "We can practice together when I'm staying with you."

"Is Dave trying out?" Beth was chagrined to have to ask. But he had told her nothing.

"Nope. He's got to get his work done. He's behind."

"That's nothing new."

Grace threw her a reproachful look. "You should try to understand. It's hard for him."

Beth was silent. She ached to cry, What about me? It's hard for me, too. But she could not bring herself to say it. It was too much like pleading.

Miss Gilles rapped for attention. "Quiet everyone! I'm going to hand around a sheet of choral lines. Read them through and try to think yourselves into them. Remember, these are poor women—devout but ignorant. The Archbishop is their protector. They know he will probably be killed, but they are powerless to prevent it. After you run through the lines silently, we will read aloud in unison. Then I will listen to you individually. I expect to cast a chorus of ten."

Beth looked around. Twenty or more students waited to try out for the chorus. Some were seniors, many were regular performers in dramatic club productions. For the first time it occurred to her she might not be chosen. And if not, her dreams of rehearsals with Ray, even private practice sessions with him, would come to nothing.

She told herself it did not matter. She didn't need Ray; she didn't need anyone. And it meant nothing to him. He was only being nice to Dave's kid sister. But her heart sank.

She scanned the handout nervously. In her anxiety, the words ran together like paint drips. After a time they swam into focus and she found herself caught up in the women's anguish, their premonitions of disaster. So engrossed was she that she was startled to hear Miss Gilles say, "Beth, you may read now."

Dry mouthed, she stepped forward. Her muscles tensed; sweat beaded her forehead. She could hear her own voice as though it belonged to someone else, someone far away. To her dismay, the words were flat and childlike; all the misery and pain imprisoned, unable to escape.

The teacher cut her off in midsentence. "Very nice, Beth. Grace?"

Heavy with shame and failure, Beth retreated. Now Grace began to speak. "Since golden October declined into somber November . . . and the land became brown sharp points of death . . ." Her voice was steady, though her hands shook so the paper rattled audibly. She did not look up; her eyes were fixed on the words.

Beth stole a glance at the teacher. She was staring at Grace. As her voice dropped into silence, she took a long breath. "Magnificent!"

No sense hanging around. No sense at all. Beth slunk away.

As she left the building, the winter day was drawing in. Lowering her head against wind-driven sleet, she battled to the subway station. She boarded a train and huddled down on the seat. Waves of misery swept her. A raucous crowd of teenagers got on at the next stop. All about her passengers drew together; Beth paid no attention. Her mind was empty of everything but the need for home. For refuge.

The trip seemed endless. By the time she reached her house, darkness had fallen. She unlocked the front door and tiptoed upstairs. She heard the clatter of Jean's typewriter from the library; she stole past unnoticed. She did not want to speak to anyone.

Safe in her room, she stood gulping back tears she would not shed. Steam hissed and clanked through the ancient radiator; she became aware that she was hot in her heavy coat. She peeled it off.

Piling her books on the desk, she switched on the lamp. It cast a golden circlet on the scarred surface. Idly she traced the lines and stains with a forefinger. The desk had belonged to Julia. With a rush of relief, it came to her that she could call her mother.

But what was she to tell her? Or Jean and her father? Or Dave, for that matter? They had all assumed she would be in the play. She had as much as told them so. How could she explain her failure? Her face burned with humiliation. She raised a hand to her forehead. No doubt about it. It was hot. Was it fever? She brightened at the thought. Flu. That was it. No one did their best when suffering from flu. She could say she had had chills. A headache. Stomach gripes. No one would blame her.

The telephone rang. Jean called from downstairs, "Beth?"

"I'm up here." She tried to make her voice hoarse.

"Pick up. It's Miss Gilles. She wants to talk to you."

Hope surged. Maybe she was wrong. Maybe she'd read brilliantly. Maybe . . .

"H'llo?"

"Beth, this is Miss Gilles. I looked for you after tryouts but you had gone. I just wanted to say how sorry I am. I know you were counting on a part in the chorus."

"That's okay," Beth said heavily. "I know I didn't read well. I knew how it was supposed to sound. I couldn't seem to get it out."

"People like us don't make good actors. We've learned to keep our feelings to ourselves."

It was comforting. She hadn't known the teacher noticed. "Thanks for calling."

"Wait, Beth. That's not all. I spoke to Miss Bardon, the music teacher. She wants you in the choir. They need altos."

"You mean I can be in it after all?" It was all she could do not to shout.

"Certainly. It's not a speaking part, but the music is important also. Of course, you'll have to fit in choir practice in addition to the regular rehearsals. Think you can manage?"

"You bet!"

"And, Beth, I just want to say we all appreciate what you're doing for Grace. You've been a good friend."

She was thankful the teacher could not see her face. Or read her mind and know how jealous she had been these past weeks.

She hung up and thundered downstairs. "Jean! Jean!"

"I'm not deaf. You don't need to shout."

"The tryouts were today. I'm going to be in the choir."

"But I thought—"

"They need altos. So I volunteered." It sounded good. And it was true as far as it went.

"I imagine you'll sing plain chant. You'll love it."

"What's that?"

"Liturgical music of the early church."

"How do you know so much about it?" Beth asked.

"I'm interested in religious art. And religion, for that matter."

"Dad thinks it's nonsense," Beth declared.

"I don't agree."

Beth stared. "Do you believe in God?"

"I'm not sure. But I used to go to synagogue regularly."

"Does Dad know?"

Her stepmother laughed. "You make it sound like a crime. I didn't marry him under false pretences, if that's what you mean. Though I'd stopped going long before I met him. Anyway, I agree with your grandmother that you and Dave should have had some religious training. If only to know where you come from."

"Dad thinks—"

"It may come as a shock, but your father can be wrong," Jean said lightly. "Though I suppose it's that assurance of his that makes him a good lawyer. As well as impossible to live with," she added in an undertone. "By the way, thanks for standing up for me the other night. I'm only sorry it got you in trouble."

There it was again. The hint of trouble between Jean and her father. "Impossible to live with." Did that mean Jean was thinking of leaving him? Beth's stomach knotted at the thought.

Once again the phone jangled. Beth answered. "How'd you make out?" Ray said in her ear.

"I'm in the choir."

"Terrific!"

"What about you?"

"I'm going to play Thomas. Did Grace get a part?"

"I didn't stay and find out. But I'm sure she made chorus. She was great."

"Super. Look, I have to go now. See you at rehearsal Monday."

Monday. She would see him Monday.

"Did Grace try out?" Jean asked.

Grace. Always Grace. Why did everyone ask about Grace?

"She's in the chorus."

"I'm glad. Robert and I will feel better if you two come home together from late rehearsals. With the dimout, there've been some muggings and holdups lately."

"When's Grace coming to stay?"

"Sunday."

"So soon?" Beth could not hide her dismay.

Her stepmother eyed her. Beth stared at her feet. When she looked up again, Jean was frowning.

"What's wrong, Beth?"

"I don't know. I mean . . . Well, Dad said it was just a trial separation. Now they're getting a divorce."

"That's what they told people at first. To give Grace time to adjust. But they'd scarcely have gone to the trouble of moving if there were a chance to patch things up."

"They used to be so happy."

Jean shook her head. "It was always a bad marriage. They weren't willing to face it."

"But I loved them!"

Jean's face softened. "You should go right on loving them. They're the same people. Just troubled. People in trouble need friends more than ever. Grace needs you. Never doubt that."

If so, Beth thought, she certainly managed to hide it. Grace gave no sign of needing or wanting her these days. She was doing fine. With Beth's friends. Beth's teachers. Most of all with Beth's brother!

"Try and be extra nice while she's here," Jean went on.

"Facing the finality of divorce is hard. As you yourself well know. Besides"— she hesitated, then appeared to make up her mind—"I probably shouldn't tell you, but . . ."

Beth went cold. What was she going to say? "Tell me what?"

"Ben's getting married. As soon as the divorce is final. He's sold the house in Philadelphia and is moving to California with his new wife and children."

"He can't do that!" Beth cried.

"Why not?"

"What will Grace do then?"

"She can visit him. California's not the end of the earth. And he'll come east sometimes to see her."

"Does she know?"

"No. And you're not to tell her. It's up to her parents."

Behind them, Dave said, "Tell who what?"

"Nothing," said Jean. "Beth and I were talking about school. She tried out for the play today."

"I know."

"How?" Beth said suspiciously. "You weren't there."

"Grace told me."

She was trying to think of a retort when he turned away, saying, "I've gotta study. I have a trig test tomorrow."

After he had gone, Beth said, "Why didn't you tell him?" Secretly she was delighted to be in the know for once.

Jean looked guilty. "I shouldn't have mentioned it. The fewer people who know the better. It's going to be hard to keep it secret with Grace here. But I thought it might help you understand."

"I won't say a word," she vowed.

Grace arrived Sunday morning with what looked like enough luggage to circumnavigate the globe. It took Dave and Robert Michaels three trips between taxi and third floor to install her with her possessions in Beth's room.

Beth watched glumly as Grace stowed dress after dress in the closet and folded her other things away in the drawers Beth had vacated. She could not help contrasting her own scanty wardrobe.

When the last immaculate item was put away, Grace flopped in a chair. "Where'll I do my homework?"

It was like her to plan for work that hadn't been assigned. Beth tried to stifle her irritation. "We can share the desk. We'll take turns."

Grace shook her head. "I need room for my typewriter. I write, you know."

"What kind of writing?"

"Poetry. And I'm starting a novel. Did you know that the Brontë sisters all wrote books before they were twenty?"

Impressed in spite of herself, Beth had to admit she hadn't. "We could borrow Jean's card table," she suggested. "There's room over under the window. C'n I read some of your poems?"

"Sometime, maybe."

"I never knew you wrote."

Grace tossed her head. "At my school in Philadelphia everyone was expected to be creative. Not like at Jefferson. All you do there is memorize."

"I thought you loved it."

"It's okay."

"Okay!" Beth exclaimed. "Only okay? After all we've done to make you feel . . . Well, the other day Miss Gilles said . . ." The words trailed off. She couldn't tell Grace the teacher had said she needed friends. Grace hated it when people talked behind her back.

"What did Miss Gilles say?"

"Just that she's glad to have you in the class."

Grace's face quivered. "She's the only one who understands."

"What about me?"

Grace rushed to her. "I'm sorry, Beth. I didn't mean to hurt your feelings. You're my oldest friend. My best friend. But that's just it. Don't you see? You have to help. Miss Gilles doesn't. So when she . . . We had a talk the other day. I showed her my poems. She thinks I have a great future in writing. Or acting." A note of importance crept into her voice.

Beth stood up. She had to get away. "I'm going down to ask Jean for the card table. You wait here."

She took the stairs two at a time. Jean was in the kitchen making lunch. "Grace settled?" she asked without looking up.

Beth was silent.

Jean put down the saucepan and eyed her speculatively. "Something wrong?"

"Grace said at her old school they had to be creative. She made it sound as if we're a bunch of morons at Jefferson. And that's not all. She had the nerve to tell me Miss Gilles is the only one who understands her. After all I've done for her!"

"Sounds as though she's got a bit of a crush on your Miss Gilles."

"On a woman?" Beth said incredulously.

"It's not unusual at your age. When I was fifteen I thought the sun rose and set with my dancing teacher. No mere boy could hold a candle to her."

Beth said sullenly, "She's not my Miss Gilles. I don't even like her much."

"I suppose," Jean went on, "it's a question of finding someone to model yourself on."

"Well, it's the other way around. It's Miss Gilles who raves about Grace. Know what she said the day of the tryouts? That Grace was magnificent."

"The point is, Grace needs friendship."

"She has us."

"No. I mean from someone she didn't know before. Someone who accepts and likes her as she is now."

"That's just what she said," Beth admitted. "She told me Miss Gilles is a help because she's not an old friend."

Jean nodded. "You don't feel so beholden to an outsider. And it's easier to tell your troubles to a stranger. You don't care so much what they think of you."

"But how come she's so down on Jefferson? Everyone there's been nice to her. Honest. Even Mr. Brown. And you know what a pill he is!"

"Do you remember Ernst Kaufman?"

"That weird refugee Dad asked to Thanksgiving last year? Sure. Dave and I couldn't stand him. He spent the whole time telling us how great things were in Germany. And how awful it is in America. Even though the Nazis kicked him out!" She stopped. "Oh! I get it. You mean Grace is like a refugee."

"Exactly. She can't quite accept what's happened to her yet. She's still pining for the old life. Pretending it was better."

The indignation died away. Beth sighed. "If only she didn't have so many new clothes. She never used to."

"Maybe that's Edith and Ben's way of making it up to her."

"Nobody ever did that for me."

"Would you really want to be in her shoes?"

"With Edith for a mother? Not on your life!"

Jean smiled at her vehemence. "I'll tell you what. You have a birthday coming soon. The first free Saturday, let's go on a shopping spree."

Beth brightened, then her face fell. "Mom might not like it. I mean . . . her feelings might be hurt if I went shopping with you. . . ." She broke off in confusion. "Oh, why does everything in this family always have to be so complicated?"

At lunch Dave said, "How about a movie? To celebrate Grace's first day here."

Beth glanced at him suspiciously. Did he mean both of them, or only Grace? He never took her to the movies.

"Super!" Grace agreed. "What'll we see?"

"*Casablanca* is playing at the Plaza," Robert Michaels suggested. "It has Humphrey Bogart and Ingrid Bergman. It's supposed to be very good."

To Beth's delight, Dave said, "I'll call Ray and ask him to come."

"Meanwhile," said Jean, "Robert and I can go and look at my new studio." Her eyes were wary.

"I thought you'd given up the idea. You haven't found a replacement for Mrs. B."

Beth tensed. Were they going to fight again?

"I'll help, Jean," Grace said. "I'm very good around the house."

"That's sweet of you, dear."

"Goody-Two-Shoes," Beth muttered under her breath. Just then Dave came back from the telephone. Scarcely daring to hope, she said, "Is he coming?"

Her brother nodded. "He'll meet us at the theater. Hurry up, you two. We can just make the two-thirty show."

It was a brilliant winter day. The sky was intensely blue, so blue it might have been squeezed from a tube of azure paint. Dave took Grace's hand. She trotted beside him, looking adoringly up into his face.

Beth set her teeth. Good will was oozing out of her like air from a pricked balloon. Not till she spied Ray waiting under the theater marquee did she regain her temper.

Inside, they found seats in the warm anonymous dark. As the music rose, Ray took Beth's hand. She was painfully aware of the hot blood pounding through his palm. Her breath quickened. She slanted a look at him, hoping he had not noticed.

She watched the movie through a haze of happy tears. At the end, when Rick and Ilse parted for the last time, she was hard put to restrain her sobs. She clung to Ray's arm as they came out into the lobby. When the light fell on her sodden face, he freed himself. Grace blew her nose loudly. Dave, too, drew apart in embarrassment.

Snuffling and gulping, Beth searched her bag for a handkerchief. Her eyes met Grace's; they were as bloodshot as her own. Without warning, the two girls dissolved into helpless laughter.

Dave and Ray closed ranks. "See you Monday," Ray muttered. Sketching a half wave, he sidled away. Dave hesitated only a moment before he strode after him.

Beth put her arm through Grace's. Still chuckling, they followed the boys up the street.

7

Rehearsals were going well. By mid-March the chorus, choir, dancers, principals, and stage crew had meshed. The play had become an organism, a self-contained world hurtling toward some unknown but inevitable climax. Outside that world nothing seemed quite real.

As Ray had promised, the gymnasium was transformed—walls shrouded with backdrops painted to resemble medieval stonework. An almost tangible weight of darkness, cold, and danger overwhelmed Beth whenever she came in. She would lift her eyes to the spotlights ranged along the balcony running track. For her, they were no longer spotlights but torches of an earlier time; in the echoing spaces of the great church she was grateful for their light and warmth. The life of the cathedral was her own now, the only one she knew. She ate, slept, breathed, and had her being in that far-off time.

The courage of the martyred Thomas was as real to her, as urgent as the struggle of Allied troops to break free of the Anzio beachhead and liberate all Italy. The battles had merged, incidents in one never-ending war for human freedom. And as time passed, the ache of rejection for the chorus lessened. What part she played no longer mattered, only that she take some part—however small.

Coming out of rehearsal one night, she struggled to explain to Ray her conviction that the words of the play were weapons. As potent as any bomb or bullet.

"It's as if Thomas were on our side. So by putting the play on, we're fighting Hitler, too." She stammered as she spoke. And cursed herself, because the words were so inadequate.

Ray seemed to understand. He put his arm about her. "I didn't know anyone else felt that way, too."

Choir practice was exacting. Beth learned to love the austere beauty of the plain chant. At night she fell asleep with the Dies Irae and Te Deum still marching through her head. She would hum aloud in the darkness. Until Grace complained, "Those songs are driving me crazy! Don't you get enough of them at rehearsal?"

In some small measure, Grace's irritation made up for the times she and Dave disappeared into his room, the closed door shutting Beth out as effectively as if they'd barred the way by force. She never learned what they talked about. Once when she screwed up the courage to ask, Grace said vaguely, "Oh, you know. Things."

True to her promise, Grace was a paragon about the house. She made her bed and hung up her clothes without being asked. After meals she was the first to leap up and clear. Though Beth suspected the alacrity was so she could reach the sink in time to wash instead of dry. A job they all detested.

"I should pay you," Jean joked. "With you around, who needs another cleaning woman?"

"If only Beth was half so willing," Robert Michaels added.

Beth gritted her teeth. But she could not stay angry long. Grace and she had been friends for too many years. And there was a lost look in those hazel eyes when she thought no one was watching. A reminder of what Beth herself struggled to forget— the breakup of her family. It was like stumbling over a garbage heap. Fly blown and festering.

Jean's wish that Grace and she come home together from rehearsals proved vain. The first few times Beth waited, only to find her friend had long since slipped away to meet Dave. Once she planted herself on the school steps, determined this time Grace should not escape. She waited an hour or more in a biting wind, feeling increasingly like a child lost in a department store.

The door banged behind her. She turned to see Ray.

"What are you doing here?" he said. "Rehearsal was over ages ago."

"I was waiting for Grace."

"Dave and she had a date at Fuller's. The soda shop on Claremont Avenue. Didn't she tell you?"

She bit her lip. "I guess I forgot."

He touched her cheek. "You're frozen. Come on. We'll ride downtown together."

At his touch a shiver ran through her. Delicious and alarming.

She was to remember that subway ride always. The grimy platform, the clanking train, the wicker seats daubed with chewing gum remained in her memory haloed with happiness.

She tucked her feet under the seat and tried to think of something to say. She was always tongue-tied with boys. Except Dave. Usually this failing mortified her. But today the silence was companionable. She was content just to be there with Ray, their bodies touching when the lurch of the train threw them together.

All too soon it came to an end. "Sixty-fifth Street," he said in her ear. "Your stop."

Grace was home before her. As usual, Beth struggled with resentment at finding her in possession of the room.

"Guess what?" Grace said.

"What?"

"Popsie called. He's coming this weekend. He wants to take us both out to dinner and a show. Want to come?"

"Are you sure? Don't you want to have him to yourself?"

Grace shook her head. "He wants to do something for you.

To thank you for being such a good friend to me."

"I'll have to ask Jean."

"I already did," said Grace, infuriating Beth all over again. "Let's pick out what we'll wear."

Reluctantly Beth moved to the closet. Grace was ahead of her—pulling out dresses, rejecting them, stuffing them back any which way.

She must be really excited, Beth thought. Grace was never messy.

"That's it!" Grace exclaimed at last. "My black. Of course I wore it New Year's, but Popsie didn't see it. What about you?"

Beth was still riffling through her wardrobe. Grace pushed her aside. "Here, let me." She eyed Beth narrowly. "You don't even seem excited."

What was wrong with her? Was it worry that she wouldn't have the right dress to wear, something grand enough for the occasion? Or was it the prospect of seeing Ben for the first time since he and Edith separated? Ben. Almost a second father. Gentler and less critical than her own. Could she be afraid to see Ben?

Grace held out the green taffeta. "How about this?"

She hadn't worn it since New Year's. She hoped it would still zip; in spite of her resolutions she had gained weight.

The week flew. For the first time since her arrival, Grace lost the haunted look. Her eyes regained their sparkle and she attacked her meals with zest. She seemed to float on a cloud of joy. To Beth's delight, she took to waiting after rehearsals instead of sneaking off. It was almost like the old days. Now it was Dave's turn to look hangdog.

On Saturday morning, Jean said, "How about going shopping with me, girls?"

Beth looked up from her oatmeal. "For what?"

"The new dress I promised you. It isn't every day you're asked on an outing like this."

Grace shook her head. "I've got much too much to do. I have to wash my hair, and shave my legs, and do my nails. I haven't seen Popsie since before Christmas."

"How did you know I needed a dress for tonight?" Beth said as she and Jean boarded a bus.

Jean smiled. "I didn't. But you seemed a bit down at the mouth. As if Grace is getting to be too much of a good thing."

"It's not that exactly. . . ."

"I know. She and Dave are spending a lot of time together. It's hard on you. You've had him to yourself till now."

"You'd think if she wants someone to talk to . . ." Beth began indignantly, "I mean, I'm her best friend."

"Dave's probably the first young man to pay her any attention."

"If only she weren't so pretty!"

"What makes you think you aren't?"

They reached their stop. In the bustle of getting off, Beth was spared the need to answer. Her steps lagged as they went into the department store. She hated to try things on. Somehow they never looked as she hoped. Each time was a fresh blow to her self-esteem. But she could not hurt Jean. Feeling as though she were led to the guillotine, she allowed Jean to steer her to the teen racks. Probably there would be nothing she liked. Or if there was, it wouldn't be her size. Or . . .

"What about this one?" Jean held a dress out.

The bodice was black, round necked and short sleeved. The skirt was fuller than any Beth had seen for some time in these years of patriotic austerity. It was boldly striped in vertical bands of black and turquoise. A wide black sash tied in the back.

"Oh!" she breathed.

"Try it on," Jean urged.

Carrying it as if it might break, Beth made for the dressing rooms. She fended off the saleswoman; she could not bear to have a witness to her disappointment.

Once inside, she stripped off her sweater and skirt and slid the dress over her head. Twisting like a contortionist, she zipped the bodice and tied the sash. Then scarcely daring to breathe, she turned back to the mirror.

Just then Jean poked her head into the cubicle. "Why, Beth! It's beautiful. You look so slim. So elegant."

"Do you really think so?" For once there was no need to ask. The mirror reflected a Beth she had only dreamed of. Tall. Regal. With soft blond hair and shining eyes.

Jean chuckled. "It would look better with pumps and stockings than those awful bobby socks and saddle shoes."

Beth grinned back. Then a terrible thought struck her. "What if it's too expensive?"

Jean examined the price tag. "Well," she said dubiously, "forty dollars is a bit steep."

"Forty dollars!" Beth wailed. "Dad will have a fit."

Jean seemed to make up her mind. "We won't tell him. It will be my treat. I've just signed up two more classes. I'm celebrating."

"By buying me a dress?"

"Why not? You're the only daughter I've got."

Beth hugged her. As she did so, she couldn't help thinking of Julia. How would she feel about it? You couldn't have two mothers at once, could you?

She clutched the precious package on the way home. For once, there had been no need to argue she would rather carry it than have it sent. She needed it that night. Jean hummed under her breath beside her. A sure sign she was happy.

As they walked up Sixty-ninth Street, Beth said suddenly, "Did you mean what you said that time?"

"What about?"

"When you thanked me for standing up for you."

"Of course."

"Well, then, why don't you ever fight back?"

Jean looked startled. "Fight back?"

"When Dad gets mad and yells. You said yourself he's not always right."

Jean was silent. At last she said, "It's not as simple as that. He can be fierce. Besides . . ." She was chewing her lip. She went on, "Oh, Beth, I love him!"

"How can you when he acts like that?"

"People can't always control their feelings. Or what they do."

"That's what Mom said. But—"

"It's not easy for him. He feels things deeply. Your mother's illness. The war. The Jewish question. It's driving him mad. People don't listen. They don't want to know. Only some-times . . ." Her voice shook; she fought for control. "Some-times I just don't see how I can cope."

Everything in Beth cried out in protest: If Dad can't help it, and Mom's sick, and you can't cope, then what are we kids sup-posed to do? But she kept silent. With all her heart she wished she hadn't spoken.

Grace was at the typewriter when they got home. Her head bristled with curlers. The radio was going full blast; a throaty voice crooned, "When the deep purple falls . . ."

Beth made a face. "How can you stand it?"

"It puts me in the mood. I'm writing a love story."

"I handed in a love story for English once. Miss Gilles gave me a C and told me to stick to things I know."

"I know all about love," Grace said smugly. "Dave and I—"

"Want to see my new dress?"

"Oh, yes! I love looking at clothes, don't you? I'll put your hair up afterward if you want. You're so clumsy about things like that."

They were ready long before Ben arrived. Beth could hardly bear to sit down for fear of rumpling her dress. When the doorbell rang, Grace ran to answer it. Beth hung back. She assured herself it was to give Grace time alone with her father. But deep down she knew she was afraid to see Ben. Would he be the same?

Then he was there. Grace hung on his arm; her eyes blazed with joy. Seeing it, Beth was suddenly afraid. She shook it off. She should be glad for her friend's happiness.

Ben came to kiss her. "Well, Beth. It's been a long time. Too long." His voice was as she remembered. Light. Amused. As though he had not a care in the world. She drew a long breath. It was still Ben. The Ben she knew and loved.

"How lovely you look," he told her. "I wouldn't have known you. You're a woman now. Not a child."

"How about me, Popsie?" Grace demanded.

"Need you ask? You're my sprite. My Ariel."

"Oh, Popsie!" Her voice wavered and she buried her face in his sleeve.

Beth turned away. To her relief, Ben said, "Come along, you two. I have tickets for the Martha Graham recital at City Center. And reservations for dinner afterward. Nothing is too good for my girls."

As their cab sped downtown, Beth could feel excitement coursing through Grace like electricity. Again she was uneasy. What would happen when the evening ended and Ben went back to Philadelphia?

She was still keyed up as the recital began. And at first the dancers grated; their movements were angular, even ugly. Quite unlike the romantic grace of *Swan Lake* and *Nutcracker*. But gradually she was caught up. It must be wonderful to have such control. Her body constantly betrayed her. So that she crept into rooms as if apologizing for her clumsiness.

There was no trace of shame in Martha Graham. Head high, she stared down the world. With the slightest turn, a mere flick of a finger, she dominated company and audience alike. Attracting and repelling at will. Her black eyes blazed hypnotically.

Had Jean once danced this way? Beth realized with a sense of shock that she had never seen her stepmother perform. Why had she stopped dancing? Had Robert Michaels forbidden it? It was impossible to imagine anyone or anything keeping Martha Graham from her goal.

By the time the last encore was over, Beth was elated. Borne up on a new resolve. She would exercise. Work even at the sports she hated. Like field hockey and basketball. She would transform her body into the instrument of her will; never again would it put her to shame. She was going to become the person she had glimpsed that morning in the department store mirror.

She pushed ahead of the others into the restaurant. As they sat down at the table, she caught sight of herself in a mirror. Her hair, disciplined to shining waves by Grace's efforts, was tousled now. And the new dress that had armored her in beauty was creased from sitting. Innocent of powder, her face gleamed. All her newfound confidence leaked away. She slumped, pretending absorption in the menu.

Unfortunately it was in French. She puzzled over *poulet à l'estragon* and *ris de veau* and *escargots*. Tears of frustration gathered in her eyes.

"Why don't I order for all of us?" Ben drawled. "To save time."

Had he noticed her confusion? She glanced suspiciously at him, but he seemed engrossed in choosing dinner. He issued a series of commands. A bottle appeared, to be placed reverently in a table-side cooler. "Champagne," Ben announced. He filled their glasses, then raised his in salute to Beth. "With my thanks for being so good to my girl."

Grace's lips curved. "To the best friend in the world," she said, and drank. Under the table her hand sought Beth's.

Beth sipped. A pleasing warmth rose in her. The wine tickled her nose and she sneezed. On a new tide of exhilaration she surveyed the restaurant. It was more luxurious than any she had ever seen. Crystal fixtures cast their glitter over brocaded walls, gilt chairs, shining napery and silver. In the center of each table was a vase with two perfect crimson roses. Their heady scent intoxicated the air.

The meal was delicious—full of new and tempting tastes and textures. It was served by two tuxedoed waiters who appeared to know just what was wanted without being asked.

Every so often, Beth glanced at Grace. The wild joy in her friend's eyes had damped to embers. Waiting to be fanned into flame again. For the first time in months she looked supremely happy.

When conversation lagged, Ben managed to supply the perfect quip or question. His eyes—so like Grace's own—rested on the two girls. As though they were the only people in his world that mattered. Basking in their approval, Beth forgot her tousled hair and dress. If only Robert Michaels would look at her that way!

"What about a breather before dessert," Ben suggested as they finished the main course. "A run around the block to shake things down. I need time to digest. Besides, I have a surprise for you."

"Tell us," Grace wheedled.

"Nope. You'll have to wait. It will only be a few minutes. Now, how's school?"

They spoke at once. "There's this play . . ."

"You tell," said Grace.

"No, you. It's your father."

Grace dimpled. "We're giving an all-school production of *Murder in the Cathedral.*"

"By T.S. Eliot?"

Her face fell. "Oh, Popsie, I wanted to surprise you. Have you read it?"

"I've seen it. It's magnificent. Are you both in it?"

"I'm in the choir," said Beth. "But Grace made chorus. Miss Gilles said she was magnificent."

His hand covered hers. "Were you disappointed not to get a speaking part?"

"At first. But now I love the music."

"She sure does," said Grace. "She keeps me awake singing in bed at night." The girls grinned at each other.

Beth turned back to Ben. He had risen to greet a tall woman advancing on the table. For one startled moment she thought it was Martha Graham. Then she saw it was a stranger. But she had the same serpentine coil of black hair wound around her skull; black eyes blazed from the gaunt face. Scarlet lips parted in a smile of greeting. Could this be Ben's surprise?

"Ben, darling! I hope I haven't kept you waiting. Now which of these young ladies is your Grace?" The gloved hand cupped Grace's chin, forcing her to look up. "Of course! I couldn't mistake the eyes. Those wonderful hazel eyes. I think they were what first made me love you." She bent, lips pursed for a kiss. Grace wrenched her face away; the caress grazed her hair.

"Girls," said Ben, "this is the surprise I promised. I want you to meet Charlotte Janeway. She was so eager to know you that I asked her to join us for dessert."

Beth's eyes met his. To her astonishment, he looked excited. Eager. As if anticipating her approval. She looked away.

Coloring, he snapped his fingers. A waiter appeared with the dessert cart.

"What will you have, Grace?"

"Nothing."

"There's floating island. Your favorite." His voice pleaded.

What did he expect, Beth wondered. Did he think we'd be thrilled? Hastily, lest the waiter take away the cart, she said, "I'll have the chocolate cake." It was seven layer. Her favorite. She dug in greedily. Then feeling Grace's eyes on her, she put the fork down again.

"I'll have an eclair," Mrs. Janeway said. She nibbled with evident enjoyment. Her teeth were white and sharp.

Ben seemed at a loss. He sipped his coffee in silence. At last he cleared his throat. "You were talking about the school play, girls. I know Charlotte would like to hear about it, too. She's a theater buff."

In a voice so shrill Beth winced, Grace said, "Are you coming?"

"When is the performance?"

"April twenty-fourth and twenty-fifth."

"Oh, Grace, I'm sorry, but—"

"Never mind. I know you're busy. I didn't expect you to come all the way from Philadelphia."

"It's not that," he said miserably. "It's . . .We hadn't planned on telling you just yet. Not this way, anyhow. But Charlotte and I are getting married. As soon as the divorce is final." He smiled at Mrs. Janeway.

"She can come, too," Grace said through set lips.

"You don't understand. We're moving that week. To California. We're starting our own law firm. And I've been asked to teach at the university. If only . . ." He made a helpless gesture.

Mrs. Janeway laid her fork down and blotted her lips. The napkin came away red. Like blood, Beth thought. She shuddered.

Grace stood up. "When did you plan to tell me? On the phone from California?"

He would have spoken, but she cut him off. "Thank you for a lovely evening. We have to go now. Robert and Jean will worry. Coming, Beth?" She started for the door.

Beth scrambled up and hurried after her.

Ben caught up with them outside on the sidewalk. "Grace . . ."

"It's all right," she said with the same deadly courtesy. "Really, I hope you and she . . ." Her voice cracked. She started over. "I hope you and Mrs. Janeway will be very happy."

"At least let me get you a cab."

As Beth and Grace climbed in, he bent to kiss his daughter. She closed the door in his face. "Sixty-ninth Street," she told the driver. "Between Fifth and Madison."

Beth whispered urgently, "Do you have enough money?"

"I borrowed ten dollars. From Dave."

They rode in silence for a time. Then Beth ventured, "It's not so bad, you know."

"What isn't?"

"Having a stepmother."

Grace said nothing. Presently Beth said, "How did you know we'd need money?"

Grace turned to look at her. In the dim light her eyes glittered feverishly. "Mummy says no woman should ever go out on a date without money. Otherwise she's at the man's mercy. 'Mad money' she calls it. I used to think she was crazy. But you know what? She was right all along!"

8

Neither girl spoke the rest of the way home. Beth racked her brains for comfort, but the words would not come. Grace's face invited neither comment nor sympathy.

As they opened the front door, Jean called, "We're in the living room, girls. Come and tell us about your evening." Beth went eagerly to stand before the fire. The flames leaped and crackled; she turned her hands this way and that in the warmth. Home had never seemed more welcoming.

Her father looked up over his spectacles. "How was it?"

Beth ached to spill her woe. But Grace was there. It was she who said, "Very nice, thank you." With that, she turned on her heel and disappeared upstairs.

Robert and Jean looked inquiringly at Beth. She struggled to begin. In the end, uneasy at leaving Grace alone too long, she only mumbled, "G'night" and fled. To find, as usual, that her friend had taken refuge with Dave.

Beth waited up for what seemed like hours, but at last she grew sleepy. As she hung up her dress, she thought with a pang of the high hopes she had set out with. She put her pumps away, for once not tossing them into the closet but aligning them side by side as Grace did. Then tired and heartsick, she crept under the covers. She did not hear Grace come in.

Julia called later in the week to invite the girls to a movie on Saturday. Relaying the invitation, Beth explained, "I think she's hurt we haven't been there lately." Though why she should apologize for visiting her mother she did not know. If Grace didn't want to come, she could do something else. Go out with

Dave. Work on her novel. If there was one. Beth wasn't so sure. Whenever she came into the room, Grace made a show of pounding at the typewriter. But the stack of finished pages never seemed to grow.

To her surprise, Grace was enthusiastic. "Yes, let's! I love Julia." It was the first animation she had showed all week. Since the evening with Ben she had been quiet. Too quiet. Instinctively Beth knew it was not the silence of despair. There were no sighs. No tears. Even into her pillow at night. Rather, there was a razor edge to Grace and all she did now. As if she had come into focus. Angry focus. As if, like a mine, she might explode on contact. Beth found herself tiptoeing around her.

Not that Grace gave cause for complaint. If anything, she was too well behaved. No hair on her head was permitted to stray. Each night she dragged the iron and ironing board from the closet and pressed a skirt for the next day, managing the most intricate pleats with ease. Her shoes were Beth's despair. She never slopped whitener on the saddles; they were as pristine as they had come from the store. Her bed would have satisfied a top sergeant. Homework was completed with dispatch; in class she answered questions with the accuracy of an automaton. She was armored in perfection, a perfection that left no opening and gave nothing away.

The worst of it was, no one seemed to notice anything amiss. Once in a while Beth caught Miss Gilles's eye on Grace; she seemed more puzzled than anxious. Robert and Jean and Dave appeared oblivious. While Beth herself was struck dumb, her growing apprehension locked within her. Sometimes she wondered at it. Was it loyalty to Grace that held her back? Yet deep within, she knew the answer. It was shame that held her prisoner. Shame at a betrayal so wounding she could not bring herself to acknowledge, much less speak of it. Because if Ben could do such a thing, might not Grace and she somehow have deserved it? Grown-ups didn't act that way. Or did they? And if so, who was there left to trust?

At dinner Friday, Jean announced, "We've heard from Edith. She'll be back Sunday. We'll take you home that afternoon, Grace. It will give you the evening to settle in together."

Beth's worries vanished in a surge of relief. To have her room to herself again! To be free of Grace's troubling presence! Then she was ashamed. Grace was her friend. Friends stood by each other.

In her agitation, she blurted out the first words that came to mind. "C'n I take dancing lessons after the play's over? I'd love to learn."

Her father raised his eyebrows. "Oh?" It was not encouraging.

"I never knew you were interested," said Jean.

"I wasn't. But we saw Martha Graham the other night. She was terrific. I thought—"

"I can't stand that woman," her father declared.

"Why not?" said Beth and Jean together.

"She's so hostile. Especially to men. It's obvious in every gesture. She's unfeminine and narcissistic. Most dancers are, of course."

A rare flush colored Jean's cheeks. "Is that what you think of me, Robert?"

He seemed embarrassed. "No. Of course not. Do you think I'd have married you if I felt that way?"

"Lately I've begun to wonder why you did."

Miserably Beth recalled the brave resolve to make herself over. Was it wrong, then? Unfeminine and narcissistic as her father said? What was narcissistic anyway?

"Why shouldn't she show off?" Grace burst out, startling them with her vehemence. "She's got plenty to be proud of. I thought it was fantastic how she made everyone do what she wanted. Just by looking at them. She was like a queen. I bet no one—no man, anyway—ever got the best of her." Her voice broke. With a stifled sob, she fled.

Dave turned on Beth. "Now look what you've done. You got her all upset."

"But I didn't mean . . ."

Jean cut in. "I'd love to have you in my class, Beth. At least someone in this house appreciates what I'm doing. Now, if you'll excuse me, I have letters to write."

Beth sat frozen, staring at her plate. After a time she began to feel queasy. How quickly food turned repulsive! The discarded chop bones might have been leavings of a cannibal feast, with gobbets of flesh and fat still clinging to them. The potato jackets resembled nothing so much as aging skin. She poked at a cold string bean with her fork.

Dave sighed. "C'mon. Let's clean up." They did the dishes in a heavy silence.

It was Tom who opened the door at Julia's the next morning. Beth evaded his embrace, but Grace hugged him, smiling at his kiss.

"Where's Mom?" Beth demanded.

"Gone to the store. She'll be right back."

He drew them into the living room. "You two get more beautiful by the day."

Grace blushed. Beth eyed her with disfavor. Didn't she see through that blarney?

"I'm hungry," she announced, stalking into the kitchen. She was standing before the open refrigerator when her mother returned, laden with parcels.

Julia looked penitent. "Pretty slim pickings, isn't it? I had no time to shop this week. We were shorthanded at the office, and I was late home every night. Besides, it seemed pointless for just Tom and me." Beth winced at the reminder of his constant presence.

Julia put the bags on the counter and reached for her. At that instant, Grace bounded in to fling herself on Julia. You'd think she was her mother, Beth thought sourly.

"Oh, Julia! I'm so glad to see you."

Julia hugged her, then held her at arm's length. "You've gotten so thin. Are you eating enough?"

"Sure."

Which, as Beth well knew, was an out-and-out lie. Grace had cut lunch every day that week. It was against school rules, but she got away with it.

As if to prove the point, Grace dug through the groceries for a cookie and drifted back to the living room still munching.

"What's wrong?" Julia whispered.

"Tell you later," Beth whispered back.

"Ben?"

She nodded. Her mother was silent a moment. Then she called out, "Let's grab a snack and go to the movies. There's a marvelous double feature at the theater on Twenty-third Street."

Beth could not but notice that her mother paid for all the tickets. Even Tom's. What did she see in him? A failure. A man without a regular job. Unless you considered decorating department store windows a job. Where did he live? How did he pay the rent? Dave's words came back to her, Where do you think he'll sleep tonight? She squirmed in her seat.

Movies usually took her out of herself. Today she found it hard to concentrate. She longed for Ray. With him she felt safe and wanted. Removed from her family's problems. Worthy of love. Was this how Grace felt with Dave?

Squashy flakes were falling as they left the theater. By the time they got back to the apartment, they were wet and chilled.

"I'll make cocoa," Julia offered.

Tom set the table. He seemed to know where everything was kept. Once again the evidence of his part in Julia's life disquieted Beth. Yet she marveled at his readiness to help, no matter how homely the task. Her father wasn't half so willing.

Julia appeared from the kitchen with a steaming pot. "Come and get it!" she cried.

It was cozy at the table. For once there were no undercurrents. Even Tom's patter was stilled. He seemed happy just to be there, sipping his cocoa and crunching fragrant cinnamon toast. Occasionally Beth caught his eyes on Julia. The look was affectionate. Trusting. Did her father look at Jean that way? She could not recall.

Grace, too, was momentarily peaceful. She downed cup after cup of cocoa and helped herself to toast and cookies without prompting. A rim of cocoa and stray crumbs lined her upper lip; she paid no attention.

It was Julia who finally broke the silence. "Jean tells me Ben was in town last weekend. How is he?"

Beth froze. Grace smiled still, but the smile had become a grimace. "Very well, thank you. He took us to a dance recital and out for supper afterward." She lifted her chin and said with something like defiance, "Charlotte Janeway met us at the restaurant."

Julia's eyes widened. "Was that the first time you had met her?"

"Yes. Popsie . . ." The clear voice faltered and recovered. "Popsie said they're getting married. And moving to California." The color drained from her face. She clapped her hands to her mouth and ran. They heard the bathroom door slam.

"Should I go after her?" said Beth.

"No," said her mother. "Let her alone. She'd be mortified to have you watch her being sick."

"Well," Tom said between his teeth, "so the great Ben Abbot has feet of clay. The bastard. The cruel bastard!"

"Tom!"

Beth knew she should be indignant. Instead she felt released. As if a tight knot in her chest had loosened. Tom was right. Ben was a bastard.

"How could he do this to her?" she demanded.

"Because he's yellow. Too yellow to tell her alone. With other people there, she couldn't say anything. Or make a scene he didn't want to deal with."

"That's enough, Tom!" Julia said sharply. "You don't know him. He's a wonderful man. Isn't he, Beth?" When Beth did not reply, she faltered, "What do Robert and Jean say about it?"

"They don't know. Grace didn't tell them."

"And you?"

Beth shook her head.

"Why ever not?"

"I thought . . . I mean, if she didn't want to talk about it, then how could I . . ." "There was a treacherous tightness in her throat. She gulped. "Oh, Mom! I didn't know what to do. Besides, Dad and Jean know all about Ben's getting married and moving. Jean made me promise not to say anything."

Her mother patted her hand. "Poor baby." She looked as though her thoughts were millions of miles away. Beth went cold. It reminded her of the dark times when Julia hadn't seemed to be there at all.

Tom pulled his chair close and put an arm around her. "It's all right," he consoled. "No one blames you. You've been a good friend to Grace. It must have been hard keeping it to yourself."

To her surprise, there was comfort in his smile and touch. She allowed herself to lean against him for an instant.

"Secrets," Julia murmured in a remote voice. "I don't like secrets. They give people too much power over you."

"Was I supposed to tell her?" Beth burst out.

Her mother paid no attention. "Your father kept secrets. He said it was to protect me. But I always thought it was because he wanted to control me."

"Julia!" Tom said warningly. "It wasn't Beth's responsibility. It was up to Grace's parents to break the news."

Julia stared at him. Beth could not interpret the look. She longed to cry, Please, Mom! Don't go back. Whatever Dad did, it was years ago. And I need you. I need you now.

Grace sidled back into the room. Not looking at anyone, she slipped into her chair. She was ashen.

"D'you want some more to eat?" Beth asked.

"I'm not hungry."

"We'd better go home. You still have to pack."

Julia roused herself. "Is your mother back, Grace?"

"She'll be home tomorrow. She has her divorce."

As they said good-bye, Julia whispered to Beth, "Take care of her."

"What do you think I'm doing?"

"I know, I know. But you can be hard sometimes. Like your father."

Everything in her rose up in revolt. She wasn't like Robert Michaels. Not at all.

Tom rode down in the elevator with them. As he stood in the snowy streect to flag down a cab, Beth noticed with a pang how shabby and thin his coat was. More like a raincoat than an overcoat really. He was shivering.

She looked back as the cab drove off, but he was gone. Had he retreated to Julia's? Or was he on his way home, wherever that was? At least it was warm in her mother's apartment. And they would be company for each other. She could not bear to think of them alone.

Robert and Jean were out when the girls got home. They found Dave and Ray downstairs in the kitchen making dinner. Ray was at the stove, wrapped in one of Mrs. B.'s old cleaning aprons. He greeted them with a deep bow. "Welcome to ze most famous bistro in Paris," he said in broad fake French. "Iz it ze smell of my cuisine zat brings two such *belles desmoiselles?*"

Beth grinned. "What's for supper?"

"Ze—'ow you call zem—'ot dogs and baked beans."

"No vegetables?" said Grace.

"Non."

"Good. Mummy makes me eat vegetables. I hate them."

"Me, too," Dave agreed.

Beth's mouth was watering. She'd had nothing but snacks since breakfast. Come to think of it, they always snacked at her mother's. Julia went into a panic when she had to produce a meal. She had been known to send out for Christmas dinner.

Ray smiled and the shabby kitchen brightened. The day's tangle of emotions—worry over Grace, fear her mother might slip back into illness, pity for Tom—was gone as if it had never been. At that instant, all that was good and true and lovable in the world was concentrated in Ray's face.

After supper Dave and Grace drifted away. Beth was unresentful. Working at the sink with Ray was peaceful. She fell into a reverie in which they were married and lived in a brownstone of their own. Upstairs the children slept. Ray was a famous actor. We'll never never get divorced, she vowed.

But with the thought, peace evaporated. Ray too seemed fidgety. "What'll we do now?" he said.

"I don't care."

"Want to listen to music?"

"Okay." Then recklessly, "Let's go up to my room."

Her heart was thumping as they climbed the stairs. She was sure he would hear it. She glanced back. He smiled; it was a stranger's smile.

When they reached her room, he stood just inside the door looking about. As if to learn more of her. She turned the radio on with fingers that trembled. A Beethoven symphony filled the air; belatedly she remembered she had left the set turned to WQXR. He would think her square. All her friends said only squares listened to classical music.

She reached for the tuning knob. Ray's hand covered hers. "Leave it."

He crossed to the bed, beckoning her to follow. Stiff with nerves, she sat bolt upright beside him.

"What are you scared of?" he said. "It's me. Remember? I don't bite."

He put his arm about her, pulling her to him. She rested her head against his chest. She wondered if he would kiss her. She ached for it. Yet remembering Bob Davidow's kisses, she was afraid. She could not bear for it to be like that.

She could hear Ray's heart pounding. He reached past to turn off the radio. She stiffened.

"Don't worry," he whispered. "I only want to talk."

"What about?" she quavered. And cursed herself. What ailed her?

"The war."

It was so unexpected that she twisted round to stare into his face. "The war?"

"I'll be drafted soon and . . ." Flushing he broke off.

Suddenly she knew, as clearly as if he had spoken, what it was he could not bring himself to say. "Are you afraid?"

She felt rather than saw him nod. The fear communicated itself; her own skin crept, her breath shortened. He was going into battle. Perhaps to be wounded. Even killed.

In agony, she cried, "Oh, Ray! Take care of yourself. Promise you'll take care of yourself."

He said nothing but his arms tightened. Whether to reassure her or himself, she did not know.

"Do you have to go?"

"You know I do. We've got to win the war. Ask your father what the Nazis are doing to our people. Do you realize that if our families hadn't come here, we would be in a concentration camp? Or dead?"

Dead. The word was irrevocable. Hard as iron. She shivered.

"And it's not only the Jews," he went on. "It's everyone. We have to fight for freedom."

"Like Thomas."

"Like Thomas," he agreed.

"I saw a movie once about the Nazis," she told him. "They even killed sick people. When I was little my mother was in a hospital. A mental hospital. If we lived in Germany . . ." She could not bring herself to go on. She had never spoken of her mother's illness to anyone outside the family before. What would he think of her? Would he still want to be her friend? She covered her face.

He pulled her hands away, forcing her to look at him. "It makes no difference," he said. "I still love you."

Their lips met. Even in her delight she was puzzled. What was it he tasted of? Then she giggled.

He tore his mouth away. "What's funny?" He sounded indignant.

Between nervous giggles, she choked out, "It's the beans."

"Better than onions," he growled. But he was smiling.

He pulled her down with him until they were prone. They lay in a happy dream. She lost all track of time.

The door opened suddenly. In the hush, the sound was startling as a thunder crack. They sprang up.

"It's late," said Robert Michaels. His voice was quiet; he might as well have shouted.

Beth prayed for Ray to leave. Quickly, before her father really lost his temper. She could not bear for Ray to hear him like that. She wasn't sure she could face him again if he did.

There was a deadly pause. Then Ray said, "See you at rehearsal Monday." He touched her hand and was gone. She could hear his footsteps on the stairs, then the sound of the front door opening and closing. She took a shaky breath.

"Don't you have any sense at all?" her father demanded. "Bringing a boy up to your room and—"

"We weren't doing anything."

"Not doing anything? I come home to find you lying in some boy's arms, and all you can say is you weren't doing anything?"

She would not look at him. "It wasn't 'some' boy. It was Ray. Dave's friend. He's good and kind and— Anyway, what about Dave and Grace? I don't hear you yelling at them."

"They're downstairs listening to records. It was they who tipped me off where you were. It wouldn't have crossed my mind. I thought you had more sense."

The betrayal left her speechless. Sick with rage, she stared at the floor. She did not trust herself to speak. She could feel his eyes boring into her. It seemed an eternity before he went away.

She was in bed when Grace came in. She pretended sleep.

"You awake, Beth?"

She kept silent.

"I'm sorry. Honest. He asked and we told him. But we didn't

mean to get you in trouble. We just didn't think."

Yeah, sure, Beth thought. So you sent him up without warning us, and . . .

Grace gave up finally. Beth could hear her tiptoeing about. At last the lights went off and the other bed creaked. The room fell silent.

Momentarily, the thought of Ray brought peace. But her mother's face obtruded, blotting out the joy and comfort of him. Julia, with that look of living in another world. A world beyond Beth's reach. Was she going to be sick again? Would she have to go back to the hospital?

That morning she had seemed angry. As though she blamed Beth. For what, Beth could not imagine. None of it was her fault. Not the Abbots' troubles. Nor their own.

Once more she told herself, I'm not like Dad. Not at all! She fell asleep with the protest on her lips.

9

Beth felt light-headed after they had taken Grace home. She had been holding her breath for weeks. Forever fearful of what might happen next. Relief left her giddy.

In the first flush of enthusiasm, her recent fears seemed over-blown. Just because the Abbots got divorced was no reason to get so worked up over her father and stepmother's squabbles. Much less imagine that her mother would be hospitalized again.

Then conscience pricked. She did not like to think of Grace's face when they left her. Edith had greeted them cordially, even brushing Beth's cheek with her lips. She was grayer and more gaunt than ever. She had strained Grace to her; Grace had stood like a stone, arms at her sides. Her mother had produced a silver and turquoise Indian necklace, saying, "Here, darling. To wear instead of the charm." Grace had thanked her, but her hand rose protectively to Ben's trinket.

And when Robert Michaels had carried in the bags, she whispered, "Thanks for everything." The look in her eyes stayed with Beth. It wasn't fair for Grace to look like that. She'd done everything she could for her. But the look haunted her still.

After supper, Dave said, "Come on up to my room, squirt. We can do our homework together."

Her heart leaped. She had him to herself again.

She flew through the algebra. Terms canceled each other out as if by magic, yielding solutions of dazzling simplicity. She was almost sorry to finish.

She looked up to meet her brother's eyes. His hair was tousled as if he'd run his hands through it. A sure sign of disquiet.

"What's up?" she said.

"I'm worried about Grace. She didn't want to go home, you know."

"No, I didn't!" she snapped, not bothering to hide her resentment. "She doesn't tell me things anymore."

"Don't feel too bad. She loves you. But she finds me easier to talk to these days. She figures you have everything straight. You get along with Mom and Jean. You have friends. The teachers like you."

She could only gape. Grace nervous with her? Grace, who had always been the leader? Who had nearly driven her crazy with her prickly perfection? Grace, who . . .

"You know how it is," he went on, "I let things go. Get to school late. Get my work in late. There's nothing about me to scare anyone. I'm forever shooting myself in the foot." His voice had hardened.

Grace and Dave. Her idols. She was speechless.

"There's Ray, too. She's jealous."

"She has you."

His mouth twisted. "Some prize. Know what she said the night before she left?"

"What?"

"That she wished Edith would have an accident and never come back."

"So she could live with Ben?"

"No, dummy. So she could live with us."

"But she loves Ben."

"Not anymore, she doesn't. Come to think of it, I'm not surprised. I never could stand the guy myself."

"Oh, Dave!"

"He doesn't seem to know or care about people at all. Not really. He just covers it over with charm."

"He was nice to me when Dad and Mom got divorced."

"So what? That didn't cost him anything. You're not his daughter. Look how he treated Grace."

So he knew about the evening with Ben. Until that moment, she hadn't been sure. Then she thought incredulously, It's Ben we're talking about. My Ben! And quick as a flash it struck her, But he's not my Ben. He's Grace and Edith's. And he left them for that woman.

As though he read her mind, Dave said, "What's she like?"

"Who?" she sparred.

He just looked at her.

She flushed. "Awful. Like a corpse with lipstick."

"Like Edith." He seemed unsurprised. "Except Edith doesn't use lipstick. Maybe if she did he might have stayed. Have you ever noticed how people seem to go for the same type every time? I fall for black hair. Dad—"

"Jean's nothing like Mom."

"Are you so sure? Neither of them stands up to him. Even though they're both career women."

"Mom's not a career woman. She works in an office."

"She has a law degree."

"Then why'd she never practice?"

He shrugged. "I guess Dad wanted her home. It's funny, isn't it? First he fell for a lawyer, then a dancer. But he didn't want either of them to do anything."

"Is that why she gets so down?"

"I don't know," he said slowly. "Dad says she had depressions long before she met him. When she was a girl."

She was silent digesting this. Then she said, "Why didn't she go back to law after they got divorced?"

"Maybe it was too much for her. All that arguing. You know how she hates to fight. It scares her. Besides, she never finishes things. As soon as she gets good at something she quits."

"Jean's not like that."

"No," he agreed. "But sometimes I wonder if Dad and she will make it." So he had noticed. And worried about it.

He must have seen her trouble, because his face changed. "I'm sorry, Beth. I shouldn't have said that. Don't worry. Nothing will happen. Honest. Only . . . Keep an eye on Grace while I'm away, will you?"

"Of course." She paused, then said abruptly, "Ray's scared of going to war."

"I know. We talked about it."

"Are you?"

"Hell, no! It'll be a relief. No more school. No homework. Just do what they tell you. Nobody can mess that up. With any luck I'll come back a hero."

She could think of nothing to say. But he had given her a mission. She would not fail him. "Leave Grace to me," she told him. "You just take care of yourself."

She gathered up her books to go back to her own room. At the door, she turned. "Does Ray . . . I mean, does he like me?" She could not bring herself to use the word love.

"What do you think?"

"You should know. He's your friend."

To her annoyance, all he would say was, "Ask him."

On the Sunday before the play, Robert Michaels announced, "Don't forget. Grandma Michaels expects us Wednesday night for Passover."

"I can't," Beth said.

"What do you mean, 'can't'?"

"We have dress rehearsal Wednesday. I don't know when I'll be home."

107

"I'm not asking, Beth. I'm telling you. Wednesday is the first night of Passover. Grandma Michaels would be devastated if you missed the Seder."

"I've canceled classes that afternoon," said Jean.

"It's not the same," Beth insisted.

"Why not?"

"Because. You have classes every day. There's only one dress rehearsal. I have to be there."

"Get yourself excused early," said her father in a voice that forbade further argument.

Dave grinned maliciously. "I have a paper due next day. . . ."

"For once in your life you can get it done early."

Beth lost her temper. "You're just trying to make it up to Grandma because we have Christmas. It's not fair. Why should I have to—"

"That's enough, you two!" Robert Michaels roared. "Leave the table."

She retired with what she hoped was crushing dignity. Dave followed her upstairs.

"That was a dumb thing to say," he told her. "Why do you always bait him?"

"How about you?" she retorted. "Anyway, it got him off your back."

"When I want help, I'll ask for it. What's such a big deal? We always go to Grandma's for the Seder. You used to like it."

"I told you. I have rehearsal."

"Talk to Miss Bardon. She'll let you out early. It's not as if you had the lead." With that he closed his door on her.

She had no more than stumbled through the first words, when the music teacher interrupted. "I know. Ray Siegel spoke to Mr. Brown. We should have thought of it. We're calling off afternoon classes Wednesday so rehearsal can begin right after lunch. You're not the only one. There are others in the same fix." To Beth's delight, she added, "I don't know what I'd do without you. You're my most dependable alto."

Despite the argument, she enjoyed the Seder. The table was festive as any Christmas tree. And the Passover dishes were old favorites. At once gay and ceremonious, with their gilt borders and ruby flowers to match the sacramental wine. Robert Michaels complained they were too fancy. Beth thought them perfect.

In past years she had been bored and restless long before the Haggadah reading was over and the meal began. But tonight the ancient tale of danger and deliverance enthralled her. She marveled at it, and at the modern miracle that kept her family safe while Jews all over Europe died.

When it came time for Dave to read his portion, she stared at him as if to memorize his face. Her brother—soon to go to fight for freedom. Like Moses. Like Thomas the Archbishop. Her stomach cramped with fear.

If only she believed in God! Then she could have prayed for still another miracle. Silently she entreated, Let him come home safe. Please. Oh, please! Though she did not know to whom she spoke.

The same prayer must have been on her grandmother's lips. More than once Beth caught her eyes on Dave, full of love and anguish. Why, she's as scared as I am, she thought. It must be awful to get old and see people you love go off to war. Maybe that's why she wears all those war relief badges. To prove she's doing something.

Aching to show her sympathy, she sang Dayenu at the top of her lungs. "Why, Beth!" Grandma Michaels exclaimed. "You have a lovely voice. You must see about lessons for her, Robert."

"I'm singing in the play this week," said Beth. "Why don't you come?"

Her grandmother bristled. "Is that the religious drama you told us about?"

"It's not religious," Dave said. "It's historical. About an archbishop who was murdered for standing up for his faith. Like Moses. And the Machabees. Please come, Grandma. Beth would love it. We all would."

"All right, David. Since you ask. But I still disapprove."

Beth jumped up and hugged her. For an instant she seemed startled; then she hugged back. Her eyes were suspiciously bright.

Robert Michaels smiled at his daughter. There was gratitude in the look.

It emboldened Beth to say, "You're like Moses, too, Dad. Trying to lead the Jews out of Europe." She felt herself redden. But a core of warmth spread through her. Could it have been the wine?

She woke that Friday with a hollow in the pit of her stomach. She felt faintly seasick. Today was the day! In homeroom, Miss Gilles surveyed the class and sighed. "I don't suppose any of you are up to serious work today. Nevertheless, you must learn self-discipline. Take out your grammars. We will diagram some sentences."

A collective groan arose. The teacher quelled it with a look. "Grace Abbot," she said. "Come to the board."

Beth turned to grin commiseratingly; when she saw her friend she drew a sharp breath. Grace was so pale she looked bloodless. Her eyes were sunken.

"Put the first sentence on the board," said Miss Gilles. "Then analyze the parts of speech, explaining as you go."

Grace picked up the chalk and began to write. Her voice was

low and monotonous. When she had finished, she laid the chalk precisely in its trough and went back to her seat.

For a moment the teacher looked nonplussed. All she said was, "Very nice. Philip, you may take the next three sentences."

Beth cornered Grace in the hallway after class. "What's up?" she demanded.

"Nothing. Why?"

"You look . . ." She broke off. Grace's face was closed. As if nothing Beth could say or do would matter.

Grace said grudgingly, "I got my period. You know I always have cramps."

"Is that all? Go to the nurse's office. She'll let you lie down. So you'll be okay for tonight."

Grace frowned. "Tonight?"

"For the play!" Could she have forgotten?

Grace nodded. Beth waited, but she stood woodenly, apparently incapable of action. Beth had to lead her to the nurse; once there she settled onto the couch with a sigh.

"Well . . ." Beth shifted from foot to foot, uncertain whether to stay or go. "I'll pick you up at five. There's supper in the cafeteria for the cast."

Through the day, excitement in the school mounted to fever pitch. Beth passed notes, and giggled, and made innumerable trips to the ladies' room. At five, she put away her books and ran for the nurse's office.

To her relief, Grace was waiting. She was still white but she greeted Beth with almost feverish gaity. "I thought you'd never come. Let's go. I'm starved."

Arm in arm, they dashed for the cafeteria. Grace wolfed her sandwiches and joined in the general banter. Beth was too excited to eat.

The gymnasium locker rooms had been pressed into service

for costuming and makeup. Beth's hands shook as she took her choir robe off the hanger. She pulled it over her head and struggled free of the enveloping folds. As the gown settled to the floor, she grew calmer. Knotting the girdle round her waist, she bent and slipped her feet into sandals.

Somewhere she had read that in the middle ages young men spent the last hours before knighting in solemn vigil. Now she turned her face to the wall, concentrating heart and mind on the drama to unfold. Because for her it was no longer make-believe, but a rededication to the cause of freedom. Like the Seder. Despite the commotion about her, she was rapt. By the time the makeup crew was done, grease paint only completed the inner transformation. She was outside herself. A wholly other person.

Grace touched her arm. She wore a simple gray dress falling to the ankles. Her hair was hidden by a hood like a nun's wimple. Framed in white, her face was childlike. Vulnerable.

"Excited?" said Beth.

"My goose bumps have goose bumps. What if I forget my lines?"

"Well, as Dave told me, it's not as if you had the lead."

Miss Gilles's voice rose above the hubbub. "Chorus and choir members get ready for your entrances. The chorus goes straight on, the choir is to wait behind the backdrop for its cue. Good luck. And remember, from now on, no talking."

"Good luck," Beth whispered.

Grace smiled tremulously. "Break a leg!" The smile faded. She was distant. Purposive.

Beth understood. This was no longer Grace. As she was no longer Beth Michaels. They were citizens of Canterbury, England, in the year 1170. Choir monk and humble woman alike, they had come to the cathedral to await the return of their exiled archbishop.

From within the great church music swelled. Miss Gilles nodded, and the chorus and choir filed in.

Waiting behind the backdrop, Beth was dimly conscious of the audience beyond. But with her fellow players she felt the strongest bond she had ever known. Women of Canterbury, clergy, tempters, knights, above all Thomas the archbishop—these were her family and friends. The only ones she had. They were her whole world.

By now the play was as familiar as a well-loved song. Yet tonight Beth listened as if for the first time. The fears of women wrenched from humdrum lives, the cautious counsel of priests, the promises of tempters offering safety and power if Thomas would but compromise, the lure of martyrdom for glory's sake—tonight she understood their terrible significance.

During the intermission, Archbishop Thomas stepped forward to deliver his Christmas sermon. Beth was never to forget Ray's voice preaching the joys of martyrdom, of dying for a righteous cause. Thinking of all those around the world who struggled and died for freedom, she trembled. Tears choked her at the archbishop's final words, " 'Dear children, it is possible that in a short time you may have yet another martyr, and that one perhaps not the last. . . .' " Please, she prayed. Not Dave. Not Ray either. Please, not anyone I love!

After the sermon, Ray exited so close to her she could have reached out and touched him. Something held her back. Tears streaked his makeup, but she could not go to him. She could only watch and wait.

In the second act, the king's knights burst into the cathedral, full of threats and bluster. Thomas refused to flee. At last priests dragged him into sanctuary, and the choir filed through the darkened church intoning the Dies Irae. Thomas broke free and, commending his soul to God, went to meet death with perfect courage. Yet in dying he triumphed, and once again the choir appeared, this time to chant the great Te Deum.

When the last words were spoken, cast and spectators faced each other in silence for a time. Then the applause began. Hesitant at first, it rose to a crescendo as the audience surged to its feet in tribute.

Beth heard a scuffling behind her. She turned to see the stage crew thrust Ray forward. This time she dared to touch his hand. He smiled briefly. Then he stood alone in the spotlight bowing to cheers and shouts of "Bravo!"

The houselights came up and the audience engulfed the cast. Beth found herself the center of an excited group. Her father's arms went round her in a bear hug. Jean shouted above the din, "Marvelous! Really professional." Grandma Michaels grabbed her hand. "I'm so glad you made me come. I cried through three handkerchiefs." Now Julia came and kissed her. Beth took a long breath. Her circle was complete.

Suddenly she remembered Grace. She looked about to see her standing a little apart. Edith was with her. Beth beckoned, but they hung back.

Julia drew them forward. "Aren't you proud of our girls? Weren't they wonderful?"

"Wonderful," Edith agreed. "I see the Michaels clan is out in full force. It's a pity Ben couldn't see his way—"

"Mummy!" Grace cried. Under the makeup her cheeks were as white as her wimple.

Undeterred, Edith went on, "But I suppose it was too much to expect. Especially on his wedding day."

"Wedding day?" said Robert Michaels.

"Didn't you know? They were married this morning. By now they're on their way to California."

"Mummy!" Grace exclaimed again. "Not now."

Julia had gone as white as Grace. Robert and Jean drew together. Grandma Michaels looked bewildered. Dave scowled and put an arm about Grace.

Edith's enjoying this, Beth thought. She wants everyone to suffer with her. But why are we so upset? We knew Ben was getting married.

Ray pushed through the crowd. "Did you forget?" he said. "There's a cast party in the library. Come on."

Beth tugged at Grace. "Let's go." Belatedly she turned to her father. "It's okay, isn't it?"

"Just don't be too late."

"I'll make sure they get home all right," Ray promised.

"Is it all right with you?" Grace asked her mother.

Edith turned reproachful eyes on her. "I don't see that I have much choice."

Beth and Ray hurried Grace away before she could respond. Beth felt nothing but relief. She was sick of the Abbots and their problems. Tonight she wanted to think about the play. About heroism and death. They were clean by comparison.

Beside her, Ray said softly, "Do you remember the night we talked about the war?"

She nodded. Her eyes searched his face.

"I just want you to know. That wasn't Thomas talking tonight. It was me. I'm not afraid anymore."

She threw her arms around him. She could not tell if it were pain or joy she felt.

"I wish it was that simple," Grace said.

Beth freed herself to turn and stare. "What?"

"Dying. It was so easy for Thomas."

Beth looked at Ray helplessly. For a moment, he, too, was speechless. Then with one accord, they took Grace's hands to drag her to the party.

10

Spring came late that year. By the middle of May, shrubs and trees around the city had only just begun to leaf out into frail green. The sight had never failed to delight Beth. This year it left her unmoved. She had been living on an exalted plane; the humdrum pleasures had lost their savor. Even the prospect of summer with its annual trek to Cape Cod was tarnished.

The last weeks of school dragged. There was the usual round of year-end class trips. Momentarily, visiting the Cloisters and the Cathedral of St. John the Divine, Beth recaptured the lost magic—imagining herself back in twelfth century Canterbury.

There was Ray, too, of course. She had to remind herself that until New Year's Eve she had known him only as Dave's friend. No more than a familiar face. Now he monopolized her thoughts, waking and sleeping. Filling the empty spaces of her heart.

On most days they rode the subway downtown together after school. He took to arriving at her house on Sundays unannounced. Occasionally they would go bowling or to the movies; more often they just sat and talked or listened to music. Generally Dave excused himself, leaving them alone together.

Beth started dance classes the week after the play. To her surprise Jean, at home too often harried and apologetic over her failings as housewife, proved dazzlingly competent. More than competent. A controlled power informed her every gesture, every movement. Watching, Beth wondered for the hundredth time why she had let herself be talked into retirement. She was as good as Martha Graham any day.

Beth limped home after those first sessions, aching in muscles she had never dreamed of. Yet with each class she gloried in a growing mastery. No one, she vowed, would have cause to label her clumsy again.

She never again discussed dance with her father. And if he was aware of her new interest, he made no mention of it. The subject was closed. Between grueling hours at the office and frequent trips to Washington, he was little at home. And when he was he seemed preoccupied, even depressed. So quiet that Beth found herself longing for him to fly into a rage the way he used to.

The one cure for his abstraction was the nightly newscast. Previously, listening to the radio with dinner had been a rare treat. Reserved for Sunday evening comedy shows like Jack Benny and George Burns. Now the radio was permanently installed on the kitchen counter. Edward R. Murrow and Larry LeSuer, broadcasting from London, were regulars at the Michaels dinner table.

At long last the war was going well for the Allies. Russia was pushing back the Germans, and the fall of Rome to Allied troops seemed imminent. The free world held its breath, waiting for the invasion of the continent. Beth thrilled to each and every victory.

She was startled to hear Dave growl one evening, "At this rate it'll be over long before I get there."

Robert Michaels laughed. A harsh bark without amusement. "Don't be in such a rush. The invasion won't be any picnic. The Germans are dug in. And even after they're beaten, there's still the war in the Pacific to be won."

"Maybe so, but I've made up my mind. I'm not volunteering for the navy. Or trying for Officer's Candidate School. I'm going to enlist in the infantry. That way I'll have a shot at going overseas and seeing action right away."

His father leaned over to pat his hand. Dave drew away. Beth knew how any show of physical affection from his family embarrassed him. More than embarrassed him. He fled from it as from a blow. When they were little, she had often teased him by pretending she was going to kiss him. It had been her only weapon against his superior size and years. Remembering those breathless giggling pursuits, she smiled. Then his last words penetrated.

"Right away . . ." she faltered. "Won't you have the summer off?"

"Whaddya mean, 'have the summer off'?"

She reddened. "Aren't you coming to the Cape?"

"There's a war on. Remember? Anyway, I told you, I'm not waiting to be drafted. I'm going to enlist right after graduation. Ray, too. We decided. We want a crack at the Nazis before it's over."

Jean intervened. "I refuse to listen to another word about the war. For once, let's have dinner in peace." She turned to Beth. "How's Grace? I never see her anymore. Not since the play. Why don't you ask her over?"

"I have. She says she can't leave Edith alone."

"Well, then, why not go there?"

Beth hesitated. She didn't want to admit she could not bear to be near Edith. Edith with her rage, her crude attempts to enlist Grace and Beth in a vendetta against Ben. Against all men, for that matter. She had even warned Beth against Ray.

"I've been hearing things about Edith recently. Disturbing things," her father remarked. "She's gotten a poor name in legal circles. It's a shame."

"What do you mean?" said Jean.

"She's acquired a reputation for being terribly aggressive."

"Isn't that a good thing in a lawyer?"

"Not when it puts people off. She's always angry. It doesn't sit

118

well with judges. Or juries. It's hard enough for a woman in the courtroom. She's on sufferance."

Jean picked her words with care. "She has every right to be angry."

"Yes," he agreed. "Ben didn't handle this well. But then, I'm not sure there is any good way to handle such affairs."

Beth tensed automatically. She did not want to listen to them arguing about the Abbots.

"Okay if I skip dishes tonight?" she asked. "I have a lot of work."

Jean nodded. She seemed to be thinking of something else. Her eyes were bleak.

Dave was hard on Beth's heels. As they climbed the stairs, he said, "Do you really have homework, or was that an excuse?"

"What do you mean?"

He chuckled. "You shot out of your chair like a scalded cat when they started in on Edith. You shouldn't mind so much. It's not your lookout."

He didn't understand, she thought. No one did.

"Anyway, if you're free," he continued, "how about giving me a hand?"

"With what?"

He looked sheepish. "The fact is, Mr. Brown lowered the boom. If I don't get those last four English papers in by Monday, I won't graduate."

"But I can't write them for you."

"All I want is for you to type them. I'll dictate. Please, Beth. You're a much better typist than I am."

Against her will, she smiled. It was rare for him to admit her superiority in anything. "Okay," she said grudgingly.

"Thanks, squirt. You're a sport."

Hours later, she straightened up with a sigh. Her shoulders

ached from hunching at the typewriter. But two of the essays were finished. She looked at her watch and exclaimed. "It's almost one o'clock!"

"Let's knock off for the night. We can finish tomorrow."

He took a lot for granted, she thought. What if she had something else to do? Why should she take him off the hook? But she knew she would.

"If I have time."

Next day she hurried home without waiting for Ray. She could hear Dave's typewriter as she bounded upstairs. She smiled ruefully. She would only have to do it over. His typing was as full of errors and erasures as a child's.

She flung open the door. "Why didn't you wait—" she began. The words died away.

Grace looked up from her brother's desk. "Hi!"

"What are you doing here?"

"Dave asked me to help."

"I already told him I would."

Grace pushed her hair back, tucking it behind the ears. It shone rich and black in the lamplight. The phrase "raven's wing" came to Beth's mind. She thought she must have read it somewhere.

She forced a smile. "Want to stay for supper?"

"I can't. Miss Gilles asked me."

"Miss Gilles?" Beth said blankly.

"I go there a lot."

"Where's Dave?"

"He went downstairs for refreshments."

Which was more than he had done for her the night before. Beth changed the subject. "How can you work without him? He dictated to me."

"I'm doing a final draft from his notes."

"But it'll be your paper. Not his."

"Who cares?" Grace said impatiently. "The important thing is that he graduates. It would kill him if he didn't."

It might well kill him if he did, Beth thought. Graduation would free him for the army. She kept silent.

"I haven't time to talk now," said Grace. "I've got to finish and get going. Miss Gilles promised she'd make something special for tonight. She's a terrific cook."

Beth withdrew, banging the door behind her. She heard the typewriter start up again. Dave appeared with a tray of milk and cookies. "D'you see Grace?" he said.

"You asked me to help!" she burst out. "I half killed myself getting home in time."

"Last night you said you weren't sure."

"I got here, didn't I? Besides, how come she can leave Edith for you, but not for me?"

He tried to placate her. "Maybe she'll stay for supper. We can listen to records afterward. All three of us," he added hastily.

"She's having supper with Miss Gilles," she told him, pleased at his shocked look.

"Miss Gilles?"

"She goes there often."

He shrugged it aside. "I guess she has a right to friends. Apart from us, I mean."

So engrossed were they that they did not hear the typing stop. The door opened and Grace stood there, eyes blazing. "Next time you decide to talk about me, how about letting me in on it?"

"I'm sorry," Beth stammered. "We didn't mean . . . I didn't know you could hear us."

"I'd have to be deaf not to! You weren't exactly whispering. I have to go now. It's getting late." With a tinge of scorn, she added, "Your papers are on the desk, Dave. Better look 'em through. Someone might expect you to know what you wrote."

Dave flushed. "Uh . . . thanks. Want me to come with you?"

"You weren't invited!" she snapped. The set of her back as she descended the stairs was a reproach.

Dave looked so crestfallen Beth took pity on him. "She'll get over it. It's not you she's mad at anyway. It's me."

"It isn't that. It's . . . Well, ever since the play she's been a million miles away. As if nothing matters. Not me. Not you." He sighed. "Like Mom in the old days when she was sick."

A pang of fear shot through her. "Oh, no!" she protested. "Besides, she loves you. I'm sure she does."

"Then why does she stay away?"

Beth cast about. "Do you neck?"

"It's hard to neck with someone who's not there. Sometimes in school we talk. But—"

"About what?"

"Nothing much."

"Who does she have, then? Everyone's got to have someone."

He shook his head. "Maybe no one. She keeps everyone away."

"It's as if she blamed us for what's happened," Beth said despairingly. She fell silent. At last she cried, "I don't get it! You'd think she'd rather have us than some old teacher." Then a thought struck her. "How'd you get her to come today?"

He smiled, but the smile did not reach his eyes. "Charity. You know. Come bail poor Dave out."

Muttering something about helping Jean with dinner, Beth fled.

Grace came up to Beth as she was leaving school next day. She looked abashed. "I'm sorry about yesterday."

"It's okay."

"No, it isn't. I didn't mean to lose my temper. Only I can't stand to have people talk about me."

"We just wanted to help."

"I know. But it's humiliating. Don't you see? Like when we were little kids and people rushed to pick us up if we fell down. God, how I used to hate that!"

Beth eyed her. "How come you never come over anymore?"

"I did yesterday."

"You know what I mean."

"I told you. I can't leave Mummy alone."

"But she works. She's never home till supper. And you haven't been to my house in weeks. Don't you want any friends?"

"I have Miss Gilles." Grace looked close to tears.

"But she's not . . ." She stopped.

"Not what?"

"Nothing."

"You don't like her, do you?"

"She's okay."

"You don't know her. She's really nice." Beth must have looked skeptical, because Grace said in a rush, "Why don't you come with me sometime?"

"D'you think she'd want me?"

"Of course. She likes you."

Beth hesitated. But curiosity got the better of her. "When?"

"Tonight, maybe."

"Tonight!" Beth exclaimed. "You were there yesterday."

"So what?"

Beth was already regretting the impulse, but she saw no way out. "I'll have to ask Jean," she mumbled, hoping against hope her stepmother would say no.

But when she phoned, Jean was enthusiastic. "Of course! I'm

happy you two are hitting it off again." Which just went to show, Beth thought bitterly, that grown-ups only saw what they chose to.

Miss Gilles opened the door to them wearing a chef's apron over her school garb of tailored blouse and skirt. Somehow it made her less formidable. She greeted the girls warmly.

"I'm so glad you've come," she told Beth. "Your friendship means a lot to Grace. And I've been wanting to know you better. I admired the way you threw yourself into the play, even though you didn't get the role you wanted. It took real maturity."

Grace plucked at Beth's sleeve. "Isn't she fantastic?" she whispered.

"Shh!" Beth hissed in embarrassment.

The teacher did not seem to hear. "Show Beth the bathroom," she said. "I'm sure you want to freshen up. It's been a hot day."

Beth looked curiously about as her friend led her down a book-lined hall and through the tiny bedroom. The bathroom was dark and old-fashioned. The window overlooked a brick wall. The few toilet articles—hairbrush and comb, a bottle of cologne, a tin of Yardley's talcum powder—were set out with military precision. Beth thought of Edith Abbot's collection.

She turned the cold tap on and splashed water on her face. Grace reached past for the cologne.

"Hey!" Beth protested. "That's hers."

"She won't mind." Grace whipped up her skirt and sat on the toilet.

Beth retreated. "I'll wait outside." The chuckle that followed completed her discomfiture.

When they came back to the living room, Miss Gilles was setting the table. She wiped sweat off her forehead with a corner of the apron. "Whew! Summer will be here before we know it. Do you have special plans, Beth?"

"We always go to Cape Cod. Only this year Dave won't be coming. He's going to enlist right after graduation."

"That will be lonely for you, won't it?"

At the sympathy in the teacher's voice, Beth's eyes pricked. She blinked hard.

"I'll be there," Grace declared.

Didn't she realize Dave was going to war? Didn't she care? Beth looked daggers at her; her friend had eyes only for Miss Gilles.

As Grace had promised, supper was delicious. Beth ate stolidly, tongue-tied and uncomfortable. Grace and the teacher seemed to inhabit a world all their own. One she could not enter. Not that they excluded her. Miss Gilles was forever asking questions, trying to draw her into the conversation. It only made her shrink into herself. The talk was erudite, witty in a way she dared not try to match. There were no familiar landmarks; it was a script without cues. "Clumsy!" she accused herself at one point, hot with shame.

Halfway through the meal, Grace recited one of her poems. When she had finished, she looked at Beth. "Well?"

Beth had not been able to make head or tail of the poem. But she would have died sooner than admit it. She was fumbling for words when Miss Gilles cut in. "Lovely," she said. "But a bit obscure. It reminds me of Emily Dickinson."

"Who's she?" Beth blurted out. At the look on both their faces, she longed to sink through the floor.

Again Miss Gilles came to the rescue. "She was a nineteenth-century poetess. Something of a recluse. She locked herself away in her rooms and saw no one. Just sent her poems out to be read."

Wasn't that what Grace herself was doing, Beth thought uneasily. With each passing week she grew more remote. More unreachable.

125

The phone rang. Miss Gilles answered; frowning, she handed Grace the receiver. "It's your mother. She seems upset."

Grace's hand shook. Without preliminaries, she said, "I'm sorry, Mummy. I should have called. Beth is here, too. What? Of course she told Jean. But— Mummy? Mummy!" The sound of the receiver slammed down at the other end was clearly audible.

"You'd better go," Miss Gilles said.

"We haven't finished dinner," Grace objected.

"It doesn't matter. She's overwrought. You should have let her know."

"I don't see why. She doesn't tell me when she's going to be late."

The teacher raised an eyebrow. "She's your mother."

They collected their belongings in silence. It was Beth who gabbled a hasty thanks. Grace maintained a sullen silence until they were on the subway.

Then she exploded. "I hate her!"

"Who? Miss Gilles?"

"No. My mother. She ruins everything. First she drove Popsie away, now she's spoiling my life. She says I can't go there anymore."

Beth said helplessly, "It's almost summer. By the time we get back from vacation, she'll have forgotten." She put a hand on Grace's arm; Grace shook it off.

"Don't you understand?" she cried. "Miss Gilles is the only one that understands. The only one I can talk to." She turned her face away.

Trying not to sound hurt, Beth said, "You have us."

"It's not the same."

"We miss you. Honest."

"You don't even know me," Grace said in a flat voice more

frightening than anger. Then she shrugged. "Oh, well. I guess you're right. She'll get over it. She doesn't care what I do anyway. Not really."

The clatter of the train wheels as they sped along seemed to be repeating, "I don't get it. . . . I don't get it. . . . I don't get it." Over and over like a phonograph needle stuck in the groove. "Want me to go home with you?" Beth said at last. "With me there she won't make such a fuss."

Grace did not reply. But as they pulled into Sixty-fifth Street, she said in Beth's ear, "Your stop. No sense both of us catching heck!"

Beth hesitated, then leaped for the platform. As the train pulled out, she caught one last glimpse of her friend's face through the window. The expression was so hopeless that Beth drew a sharp breath. Then her eyes blurred; turning, she stumbled toward the exit.

he first week in June was breathless, as hot and muggy as the dog days of August. Beth came home from school that Wednesday to find the whole house hunkered down for siege — shades drawn against the sun, rugs rolled up and pushed back to the walls, furniture swathed in faded seersucker.

She kicked off her shoes and socks and scuffed her feet luxuriantly against the bare parquet. Then she ambled down to the kitchen for a Coke. She was slurping the last tangy bubbles when Jean got back.

"Hi!" Beth greeted her, suppressing a burp. "You're early."

Jean mopped her flushed face. Her curls were plastered to her head with sweat.

"Thank God, that was my last class for this year! The studio was so hot I thought we'd all pass out."

"There's another Coke in the fridge. Want me to get it for you?"

Jean nodded. She took a long swig from the bottle and hiccuped. She looked so startled, Beth had to laugh.

Jean giggled, too. "It's the bubbles. How was school?"

"Awful. We opened all the windows but it didn't help. Even Miss Gilles complained. And she never admits anything bothers her. I bet if she was caught out in the desert in a fur coat, she'd say she wore it to keep off the sun."

"I just hope it cools down by the weekend. Graduation is Friday and Dave only has the one suit. It's not exactly summer weight, but there seemed no point in buying a new one. He'll probably grow two sizes before he gets back."

If he gets back, Beth thought gloomily. There was no getting away from it. Dave and Ray were going to war. Nothing would ever be the same again.

"That reminds me," she said as brightly as she could, "Grace wants to come to graduation with us."

"Of course. What about Edith? Shall I ask her, too?"

"I don't think Grace would like it."

Jean looked startled but all she said was, "I've invited Grandma Michaels to dinner that night. And Julia. We'll go together."

"Can't Mom get there on her own for once?"

"Beth!"

She was already regretting the outburst. "I just don't like it when she's here," she muttered.

"It's awkward," her stepmother agreed. "But at least she and your father don't fight."

Beth thought of Edith. "I guess so," she said reluctantly. "Only it seems so fake. I mean, everyone pretending nothing's happened and . . . I guess I just like Mom better at her place and you and Dad here."

"A place for everything and everything in its place? The trouble is, life's not like that. All neatly packaged. Anyway, it's not phony. Not the way you mean. Your father likes and respects Julia. And so do I."

Yeah, Beth thought. But how does Mom feel seeing you here with her husband and kids? I'd murder anyone who tried to take my place with Ray.

Friday came all too soon. For Beth, the last day of school was tinged with melancholy. Her brother and her boyfriend were going to war. The words reverberated like the lyrics of some sad song.

Even an unexpected B in algebra did nothing to allay the

ache. She cleaned out her locker in a fog of misery—unearthing two mislaid term papers, a sweater lost since February, two library books, and a collection of orphan mittens.

Beside her, Grace said, "Want to ride downtown together?"

"I promised Ray."

"Okay. I'll go find Miss Gilles. See you tonight."

Beth wanted to cry after her, Don't you want to come home with Dave? You might never get another chance. He may be killed.

An arm fell across her shoulders. "Let's take a last look at the gym," Ray said.

They fought their way upstream against a tide of laughing, jostling students all making for the exits. When they reached the gymnasium the janitor was just pulling down the window shades. The equipment was already pushed back to the walls. The great room was deserted. Ghostly.

" 'Now is my way clear, now is the meaning plain,' " Ray said softly.

Beth stared. Then it came to her. They were the words of Thomas Becket.

In the same faraway voice, he went on, " 'Now my Good Angel, whom God appoints to be my guardian, hover over the swords' points.' "

Her heart lurched. He was saying good-bye. To her. To school. To the magical world they had shared for so short a time. Silently she amended the prayer, Hover over the guns' points!

When she could trust her voice, she whispered, "Ray?"

He scarcely seemed to hear. But at last he blinked and shook himself, as though waking from sleep.

"Ray!" she said again, and threw her arms around him. "You'll come back!" she promised. More to convince herself than him.

130

"We'd better go," he said in his normal voice. "I have to get ready for graduation. And we're having supper early."

"Your parents are coming, aren't they?"

"Of course."

"Good. I want to meet them. I missed them at the play."

"They didn't come. They don't go in much for that kind of thing."

"Why not?" Seeing his face close, she said quickly, "I guess they're like my grandma. She thought it was a religious play. She almost didn't come either."

He shook his head. "It's not that. They're socialists. They don't care about religion. It's their English. Mostly they get along fine, but Eliot isn't easy. Besides, they don't really approve of my acting. Where they grew up, actors were entertainers. Not artists."

"Where do they come from?"

"Russia. They escaped just after the revolution. My father had trained to be a lawyer. But here he writes for the Jewish press. He and his friends talk more Yiddish than English."

"My father's working to get Jews out of Europe," she told him.

"I know." It was so curt she stared. Was he angry about the night her father had found them together?

She pondered it all the way home. She was still pondering as she bathed and dressed. When she came downstairs she found her mother in the living room with Jean and her father. As always, their small talk made her feel like a cat stroked the wrong way.

But she eyed her mother with approval. Julia wore a new dress; she was almost pretty in the bright summer print. Her hair was freshly done, piled high on her head. If she shared Beth's fears for Dave, they were hidden under careful makeup that lent color to her normally sallow cheeks.

Beth dropped a kiss on her head.

Julia smiled at her. "How nice you look. Where's Dave?"

"Still in the shower. You know him. He'd be late to his own funeral." The frozen pause told her what she had said. She could have kicked herself. This was no time for flip remarks about Dave and funerals.

Robert Michaels put his glass down. The highball slopped over. "Will that boy never learn to be on time?"

Jean and Julia spoke at once. "Now, Robert . . ."

Beth found her voice. "Why can't you leave him alone?" she blazed. "It's his graduation. Not yours."

He rounded on her. "One more word out of you . . ."

The doorbell rang. "That's Grace," Dave called from the stairs.

"I'll get it," Beth cried, and beat a hasty retreat.

Grace and Grandma Michaels stood on the step. Grandma Michaels seemed bemused at the welcome, but Grace brushed by to embrace Dave. As if making up for past neglect.

In spite of Jean and Julia's efforts, dinner was a strained affair. But the atmosphere lightened as they set off for school. The auditorium was crowded when they arrived; the last seats were in the kindergarten section. Grandma Michaels lowered herself into the tiny chair with a grunt. She was so tightly wedged Beth wondered how they would extricate her.

The orchestra struck up a ragged "Pomp and Circumstance," and the class of 1944 filed on stage. At that moment a large woman sat down in front of Beth and her grandmother. She wore a huge straw cartwheel hat trimmed with fruits and flowers. Beth craned her neck to see past. She was beginning to despair when Grandma Michaels leaned forward and tapped the woman on the shoulder. "Will you kindly remove your hat?" she said in a carrying voice. "I can't see my grandson."

Beth blushed. The woman turned to glare, but Grandma Michaels stood her ground. Grumbling, the woman took off the hat.

"Gee,thanks, Grandma," Beth whispered.

"Not at all. I was afraid the vegetation might attract insects. Most unhealthy!"

Jean stifled a chuckle.

Beth spotted Dave and Ray. Satisfied, she swiveled round to inspect the audience. Perhaps she might identify Ray's parents. They would look like him, of course—tall, blond, and distinguished. Would his father have a beard? In movies, Russians often did. She rejected the idea. Too scratchy.

Mr. Brown stepped to the rostrum. Beth yawned. Her hand flew to her mouth but a small yelp escaped.

"Beth!" chided her father.

"I can't help it, Dad. He's so boring."

Her father grinned. "That bad? Sounds like one of the senior partners at my firm. He sends me off whenever he opens his mouth. It's too bad we can't patent it. Much cheaper than sleeping pills."

The principal cleared his throat and began to speak. He seemed to be reading from a list. Beth's attention wandered. The auditorium was stifling and her eyelids drooped. Suddenly she jerked to attention. About her, she heard sniffles and frank sobs. Grandma Michaels pressed a handkerchief to her lips. The truth burst upon Beth. These were the names of Jefferson graduates killed in the war. Her own throat tightened.

Mr. Brown laid aside his spectacles and looked up. "Now let us all observe a moment of silence for these brave young men who gave their lives for freedom. And let us offer up a prayer for those who graduate tonight into a world at war."

Silence fell over the packed hall. Even the tears were stilled.

Beth hardly dared breathe. It seemed an eternity before the principal raised his arms. As one, the audience rose and the orchestra swung into "The Star-Spangled Banner."

As the last notes of the anthem died away, Mr. Brown signaled and one by one the seniors filed past to receive their diplomas. When Ray's turn came, Beth clapped till her palms stung. Out of the corner of her eye she saw a couple in the next row stand and applaud. She blinked in disbelief. Those couldn't be Ray's parents! Ray was tall and blond. So handsome it hurt sometimes to look at him. While these two were dumpy and graying. Even at this distance she could see the man wore thick glasses. His ill-fitting suit shone with wear. His wife bulged in her shabby summer frock. Her face was innocent of makeup.

There was no time for wondering. Beside her, Grandma Michaels exclaimed, "There's our David!" And they all clapped again.

There was a reception in the library after the ceremonies. For once, Dave endured their embraces without flinching. Beth's eyes strayed, searching for Ray and his parents. At last Dave whispered, "They're out in the hall."

She found them awkwardly balancing punch cups and cake. They looked hot and uncomfortable. Ray towered over his parents. When Beth appeared, he put an arm protectively about them. He seemed unsure whether he was glad to see her.

Feeling like an intruder, she said, "Hi!"

"You are the Beth we have heard so much about?" said Mr. Siegel in heavily accented English.

Before she could reply, Mrs. Siegel darted forward to enfold her in her arms. Tears trickled down her cheeks.

"Mom!" Ray exclaimed. "Don't cry. You'll embarrass Beth."

Mr. Siegel disentangled his wife, patting her shoulder and crooning, "Now, Ruthie. Don't cry so. Our boy will come back to us."

Glaring, she freed herself. "My Raymond goes to war and you tell me not to cry? What kind of father are you?"

Ray was scarlet. He looked imploringly at Beth.

To her own surprise, she hugged Mrs. Siegel and whispered, "I know how you feel. My brother is going, too. But they'll come home. You'll see."

Unexpectedly, Ray's mother laughed. More a giggle than a laugh. High and bubbling like a girl's.

The men eyed her suspiciously. "What's so funny?" Ray demanded.

"It's . . ." She could not go on. Again tears flowed; this time they were tears of laughter. At last she gasped, "Your Beth will think we're all meshuga."

"Meshuga?" Beth repeated. She looked at Ray inquiringly.

"That's Jewish for crazy," he told her.

"Oh. I thought maybe I'd said something wrong."

Mr. Siegel took her hand. His grasp was warm and firm. "You'll come to see us after Ray goes?"

She nodded. "I'm going to Cape Cod for the summer. When I get back . . ."

An undemanding silence fell. Beth wondered how she could have imagined them other than they were. She made no move to take her hand away.

Mr. Siegel sighed finally. "Come, Ruthie. It's a long subway ride home."

"You could get a cab on Broadway . . ." Beth began. And stopped. Because they did not look as if they took taxis often.

Mrs. Siegel chuckled. "I get my exercise running for trains. So one day maybe my dress will fit like it used to." She patted Beth's cheek. "Don't make yourself a stranger. Come. We'll have a glass of tea and talk about Raymond."

Yes, Beth thought. She would go. It would be comforting to have someone to talk to about Ray.

As they turned to go, she said hurriedly, "Wait! You haven't met my parents."

She saw a look pass between them. They seemed embarrassed. "Your father is a fine man," said Mr. Siegel.

"Oh, have you met him?"

"I heard him speak once. At a meeting."

She thought he would say more, but he bit off the words. His face had darkened.

"Avram," his wife cautioned. "Not tonight. Tonight is for happiness. Our son has graduated from a fine school."

"I know." He smiled at Beth. "One day, perhaps, your father and I will meet. And who knows? I may convince him that after the war is won, we Jews must work together to build our own land. In Palestine."

Ray tugged at his arm. "Another time, Dad. We have to take Mom home."

Beth said forlornly, "When am I going to see you? You leave Monday."

"I'll come over to your house later. After I take my folks home."

She felt bereft as they walked away. Ray and his father flanked Mrs. Siegel; they pressed close together.

Dave and Grace ran up. "Did Ray leave?" said Dave.

"He'll be over later. He's taking his parents home first."

"I'd better catch him. Grace asked us up to her place." He was off before she could say a word.

Her heart sank. She had dreamed of her last minutes with Ray. Now it seemed she was to share them. She did not want to spend the precious time with Grace and Edith.

To her relief, Edith was nowhere in sight when they arrived. Grace hustled Dave out to the kitchen to collect the refreshments. "We've got cheese and crackers. And Mummy promised to leave a bottle of champagne on ice. For a treat."

Beth drew Ray into the living room. He whistled. "What a place!"

Unaccountably defensive, she urged him out to the terrace. As they stepped outside he whistled again. She felt for his hand. Together they moved to the railing to look out over the enchanted scene. Suspended in a velvet sky the moon hung like a globe, etching skyscrapers and tenements alike with silver splendor. Along the streets and avenues below, traffic picked its way—dimmed headlights flickering like fireflies in the night. A tiny breeze ruffled the terrace greenery in its pots.

Beth shivered. Ray put his arm around her. "Cold?"

"No. It's just too beautiful."

He drew her closer. She sighed. Whatever happened, they would have this to remember always.

Behind them the French doors opened. Beth turned to see Grace carrying a loaded tray.

"Are you going to help, or just stand there necking?" Grace's voice was hostile.

Before Beth could reply, Dave appeared with the champagne. Grace slammed the tray down on the table and lit a hurricane lamp. The candle flame leaped and guttered.

Ray broke the silence. "With a terrace like this, who needs to go away for vacation?"

Grateful for the diversion, Beth said, "I thought you were going to put in a garden."

"We didn't get to it," Grace snapped. "Mummy's never home."

They relapsed into speechlessness. Beth put out a tentative hand to the refreshments and withdrew it again. Dave stubbed out his cigarette and went to lean over the rail.

"Come back!" Grace cried. "You'll fall."

He laughed. "Don't be silly."

"Please!" Her voice was shrill.

Beth leaned forward, peering through the gloom. Her friend's face was contorted with fear.

Grace said shakily, "I'm terrified of heights. I've never even been up the Empire State Building."

"There's a guardrail," Ray said.

"I know. But even looking up at tall buildings makes me dizzy. I always think they'll fall on me. They move."

"That's just the motion of the clouds."

"You'll think I'm nuts," Grace went on, "but sometimes I wake up at night with the room tilting. I have to hang on to the bed to keep from sliding out the window."

"Even when it's closed?" Beth quipped.

Grace threw her a look. "Sometimes I wonder what it would feel like."

"What?" Dave said impatiently.

"Falling. I mean . . . would you drift down like a feather or explode like a bomb?"

"Just don't try it," said Beth. "You'd make an awful mess. Like the 'big black bug that bled blood on the barn floor.' "

Grace joined in the general laughter.

"Tell you what," Dave suggested, "take my hand and we'll walk over to the edge together. It's safe. You'll see."

Grace froze. Then without a word, she wheeled and went back inside.

There was a painful pause. Dave muttered finally, "I wish I knew what's eating her. I asked her to the Village Vanguard for a jazz concert. But she wouldn't hear of it. She said she had to throw a party. Some party!"

"She's upset about your leaving," Beth said, trying to console him.

"She's got a mighty funny way of showing it. First she won't come near me, and when she does she's spoiling for a fight. I can't seem to do anything right. We had a blowup back there in the kitchen. I offered to help, but she wouldn't let me touch a thing. I thought maybe the champagne would cheer her up, but—"

"I'll go see if she's okay," Beth said.

"Better let me."

When he had gone, Ray said, "Thanks for being so nice to my folks."

Stung, she retorted, "I wasn't being nice. I liked them. Didn't you think I would?"

He looked embarrassed. "They're different from the people you know. They have an accent. Their English isn't perfect. Did you mean it when you said you'd visit them?"

"Of course."

"Because it would mean a lot to them. They don't have many people. I'm all the family they've got. Dad's relatives were all killed in the revolution. And we haven't heard from Mom's folks since the Germans invaded."

Thinking of her father's tales of German savagery, she shivered again. "We're lucky to live here."

"And how!"

"What did your father mean about Palestine?"

"He's a Zionist."

"What's that?"

"Don't you know anything about being Jewish?"

The darkness hid her flush. "Not much. You see, my father thinks—"

He brushed this aside. "Zionists believe Jews will never be safe until they have a country of their own. A homeland."

"We have a home. The United States. We're American."

"German Jews thought they were German. Look what's happening to them."

"But my father says—"

"I know what he says," Ray said with a touch of impatience. "He wants the Jews to come here. Or to England."

"What's wrong with that?"

"Nothing. Except that England and America don't want them. They've made it as hard as they can to get here. They haven't lifted a finger to help. And even when the war's over, there's no guarantee it won't happen again."

"My father—"

He looked uncomfortable. "Look, Beth, I don't mean to criticize. He's fought a terrific fight. But it's a losing battle. My father and his friends on *Der Tag*—the Jewish paper he writes for—are thinking ahead. They know there's not much to be done to save the people in concentration camps. But they want to make sure Roosevelt and Churchill allow the survivors to go to Palestine after the war."

"What if they don't want to? I wouldn't. I love America. It's my home. I don't believe it can happen here."

"You know that meeting where my dad heard your father speak? They had an argument. The same one we're having now," he said sadly. "That's why my parents left without meeting yours. They didn't want to get into a fight at graduation."

"It won't matter to us, will it?" she cried. She could not bear for them to fight. Not tonight. Not ever.

For answer, he took her hand and led her to the glider. Pulling her with him, he slipped down. She stiffened, then relaxed. He cupped her chin with his hand, turning her face so he could kiss her. She kissed him back, holding him fiercely to imprint the feel of his body on hers. Lest he slip away forever.

His breath came faster. His lips bruised hers; his tongue forced her mouth to open. His hands were gentle on her breasts. A wave of gratitude swept her.

Without warning, he wrenched himself loose and stood up. She gave a small involuntary cry. "Don't stop!"

"I'm sorry," he muttered. He would not look at her.

"Please, Ray. It's our last night."

He shook his head. "I shouldn't have started this. You're just a kid."

"I'm not. I'm not!"

"Come on," he insisted. "I'll take you home."

Close to tears, she followed him back into the living room. Dave and Grace were sitting at opposite ends of the white couch. The phonograph wailed.

Beth slid her hands down over her rumpled dress. She dared not meet her brother's look.

"You leaving?" he said in surprise.

"It's late," Ray replied.

Dave looked at Grace, but she was silent. "Guess I'll go, too," he said. Still she did not speak. "I probably won't see you again before I go."

With one sinuous catlike motion, Grace uncurled herself and went to turn off the music. The record squawked and died.

Grace padded barefoot into the foyer and stood waiting at the door. She held out her hand. "Bye, Dave. Good luck and thanks for everything."

He bent to kiss her, but she shrank away. "See you," she said, and closed the door on them.

12

Beth woke the next Monday to a premonition that something unpleasant was about to happen. She lay blinking up at the familiar stain on the ceiling over her bed, trying vainly to track down the source of her discomfort.

Suddenly she remembered it was the first day of vacation. She didn't have to get up yet. She rolled over onto her stomach, burrowing under the covers to shut out the light.

But sleep had fled. Her unease mushroomed; each and every nerve seemed charged with electricity. Why did they call it butterflies in your stomach? It felt more like cockroaches crawling over you.

The door opened. She closed her eyes and took long regular breaths.

"Beth?" said her father. "Beth!"

Reluctantly she turned her head to squint up at him.

"Time to get up."

"It's vacation. There's no school."

"Don't you want to say good-bye to Dave?"

With that, memory flooded back. Today was the day she had dreaded. Today Dave and Ray were to leave for the army.

"There's something else, too. It's begun."

She struggled into a sitting position. "What has?"

"The invasion. Allied troops are landing in Normandy."

A thrill ran through her. "I bet Dave's furious not to be there."

"Well, I'm damned glad he's not. The casualties must be terrible. But it's the beginning of the end. If only . . ."

She squeezed his hand. "You're thinking of the Jews, aren't you?"

He nodded.

"Won't they be all right now?"

"Oh, Beth! So many have already died. And many more will be slaughtered before we reach them."

"What about Palestine?" she ventured.

He smiled wryly. "You've been talking to the Siegels, haven't you?"

"Do you care?"

"Of course not. You must make up your own mind."

"Well, then . . ."

"For most European Jews there's no more chance of reaching Palestine than coming here. But we'll talk about it later. Dave's having breakfast. If you want to say good-bye to him, you'd better get a move on."

It touched a raw nerve. She could not bear to see him go. If only she had overslept! But her father's eyes were on her. She stumbled out of bed and downstairs.

Dave was at the kitchen table. He looked up from his cereal. "Have you heard?" he said, wiping the milk from his upper lip. He was hoarse with excitement.

"Dad told me."

"God! I wish I was there."

She gave him a wan smile, but she felt more like crying. "Where do you go first?"

"Downtown to Whitehall. Then to Fort Dix, New Jersey, for processing. I don't know where they'll send me for basic training."

"Oh," she said in a small voice.

"Don't look so tragic. I'll be home before you know it. The war can't last much longer."

She swallowed. "Is Ray going with you?"

"To Fort Dix, I guess. After that who knows?"

"You mean you won't be together?" It was a cry of dismay.

He seemed puzzled. "It would be nice to have a buddy there. But that's my problem. Not the army's. What's it to you, anyway?"

How could she explain what she herself did not fully understand—the conviction that together they would be safe? While separated they would escape the watchful orbit of her scrutiny. Drifting off into oblivion to be forever lost.

"Time to go, son," said Robert Michaels.

"Right, Dad."

Their father held his arms out, then let them drop. Dave shook his hand. At that moment Jean flew downstairs to hurl herself at him. He gave her a gingerly kiss.

Beth grabbed his arm and hung on. "Try to stay together, you and Ray. Promise?"

All he would say was, "So long, squirt. Take care of things for me."

He slung his duffel over his shoulder and strode down the hall. He looked anxious to be off. At the door he called back, "See ya!" It banged behind him and he was gone.

Beth and her father stood frozen. Jean urged them back to the kitchen. "We'll all feel better for breakfast." She got eggs and bacon out of the refrigerator and banged the frying pan onto the burner with unnecessary force.

Beth slumped on her chair, stunned with loss.

Her father cleared his throat. "I suppose . . ." The words trailed off. He seemed to have forgotten what he meant to say. He switched on the radio.

The newscaster's voice filled the room. "Despite stiff resistance, troops and supplies continue to pour ashore in Normandy. As yet there is no official word on casualties, but—"

There was a click and silence fell. Startled, Beth looked up. Her father seemed bewildered by his action. "What are your plans for today, Jean?" he said in an attempt at conversation.

"Errands. I have some last-minute things to pick up for Beth to take to the Cape tomorrow. After that . . ." She lifted her chin defiantly. "I'm going to Temple Emmanuel. To pray for those boys on the beaches. And Dave."

Beth held her breath. But all her father said was, "Can't do any harm." He turned to her. "What about you?"

"I have to pack."

"That reminds me. Grace is driving up with you and Julia tomorrow."

"I thought she and Edith weren't going till next week."

"Edith's not going. She says she can't afford the time away from work." He frowned. "As usual she blames it on Ben. But I think she just can't face Cape Cod this year. Too many associations."

"Where will Grace stay?"

"With us, of course. Or rather, with you and Julia. By the time Jean and I come in August, she'll be heading for California to visit Ben."

"But . . ." She tried and failed to hide her dismay.

"I thought you'd be delighted. She'll be company for you with Dave not there. Hasn't she spoken to you about it?"

"No."

"That's odd. I'm sure Edith told her. She asked me weeks ago, and I talked to Julia right away. She was very pleased. She suggested Grace could use Dave's old room."

"Haven't you two been getting along?" said Jean.

"She's funny these days. You know. Funny 'weird.' Not funny 'ha-ha.' "

The telephone rang. Beth answered. Grace said in her ear, "Have you heard the news?"

"About the invasion?"

"Uh-huh. I'm petrified for Dave!"

And if you believed that, Beth thought, you'd believe in Santa Claus. She'd practically thrown Dave out of the house graduation night. She said reluctantly, "Dad says you're coming to the Cape with us. It'll be great."

"Do you mean it?"

"Of course." To her ears it was unconvincing.

"I was afraid to mention it. I thought you were mad at me."

Suddenly she was exhausted. She wasn't sure her legs would hold her. All she wanted was to creep back to bed and howl into the pillow. "See you tomorrow," she mumbled.

Packing took the better part of the day. In the past, she had hurled things into her suitcase. Today she moved as if underwater—sorting, discarding, choosing with infinite care. The room looked uninhabited when she was done. As if no one lived there. She might have been going away forever.

The house was quiet. Too quiet. Only the maddening drip of the leaky faucet in the bathroom broke the hush. She closed the last bag and rose from a half crouch to drift along the hall and stare into Dave's room. It was as lifeless as her own. She felt ghostlike, disembodied.

The whole day passed in that unnatural silence. When the front door banged, Beth went thankfully to help Jean with dinner. They moved about the kitchen unspeaking, unable to think what to say. Her father came home at last; the three of them huddled around the table like refugees.

Far into the night, Beth could hear the radio in her father and stepmother's room below. "Allied forces are struggling to deepen beachheads all along the Normandy coast." She was thankful for the insistent voice. She and Dave had shared the third floor. Tonight she was alone for the first time.

Hours later she woke from an uneasy sleep, sweating with terror over nightmare visions of Dave and Ray swimming ashore into a hail of bullets. She told herself they weren't overseas yet, much less in action. But she lay wakeful the rest of the night. She thought of Ray's last phone call. He had sounded preoccupied. Trying and failing to hide his eagerness to go. Poised between their world and one she could neither enter nor share.

Long before a hazy dawn filtered through the shutters, she was impatient to get away. She took a cold shower, threw on her clothes, and went downstairs, suitcases bumping against each step.

Her father was making coffee. His face was haggard; she wondered if he, too, had been unable to sleep.

"Want me to stick around?" she offered. "I could go by train next week."

"I'll be all right," he said. "Have you forgotten your mother? She needs you. Dave's going is as hard for her as it is for me. Harder maybe. I have Jean."

Fighting resentment at his brusque dismissal, she got out a bowl and filled it with cereal. She reached for the milk.

"Watch what you're doing," her father warned.

She looked down. Milk was spreading in a pool around the bowl. She had a sudden vision of the time when she was small and had poured out an entire quart on the table. In a fit of naughtiness. Her mother had been in the hospital at the time. Her father had smacked her hard. The delicious mix of terror and pleasure was with her still. She wondered if that was how men felt going to war. Licensed to do their worst. To kill even.

She shoveled cereal into her mouth. By now it tasted like wet hay.

"Slow down," said her father. "What's the rush?"

"You know Mom. She's always early."

But she waited for almost an hour on the stoop before the old black Pontiac turned the corner. She held her breath as her mother maneuvered in to the curb. Julia was not noted for her driving skills. Once, at the Cape, she had dented all four fenders in succession turning behind the garage. Today she parked without mishap.

To Beth's astonishment, two people sat on the backseat. She had expected Grace. Who was the other? She galloped down the steps and stuck her head in the window. Tom Duffy grinned at her. She scowled. Was he coming, too?

There was no time for questions. Her father was on her heels. He crammed her bags into the trunk and came around to the driver's side.

"Sorry I'm late," Julia apologized. "The traffic was fierce. You'll be sure and let me know the minute you hear from Dave, won't you?"

"Of course. Have a good trip and take care of yourselves." He sketched a wave and turned back to the house.

The farewell left Beth desolate. All the way up the Post Road and through the noonday crush of Providence, the others laughed and bantered. She made no effort to join in, even refusing the picnic lunch her mother had brought. They don't care that Dave's gone, she thought. Even Mom. So long as she has her precious Tom, everything is okay.

She twisted round to demand, "What are you doing here?"

Tom smiled at her. "Julia invited me to spend a few days. It will be a bit of a vacation for me, and I can help with the heavy work. Things Dave used to do. Like putting the boat in the water."

It only served to fuel her resentment. Grace was to sleep in

Dave's room. Tom would do his chores. It was as if he had died!

She reached for the radio switch. Her mother stopped her. "Don't! I can't bear to listen to the war news. What if Dave were there?"

Remorse assailed Beth. While she sulked, her mother agonized. To make it up to her, Beth said, "I bet the war's over long before he gets there."

Julia turned beseeching eyes on her. "Do you really think so?"

Beth's mood lightened as they crossed the bridge onto Cape Cod. Happily she pictured the strip of white sand sloping down to the water near their cottage. She could almost feel it, sun warmed and powdery between her toes. In the rearview mirror her eyes met Grace's. And suddenly it was all right. They were home. Home on the Cape where they had shared so many happy summers.

Anticipation built as main roads gave way to lanes bordered in scrub pine. Rambler roses covered the fences around weathered cottages. Signposts told of places Beth had known and loved since childhood: Sandwich and Barnstable, Falmouth and Hyannis, Centerville, Cotuit, Mashpee and Poponesset.

"Some of them are Indian names," she told Tom, forgetting her resentment in the joy of return.

It was midafternoon before they turned into the track leading to the cottage. Julia pulled up at the garage in the rear of the house and they got out. Beth inhaled deeply, savoring the mingled tang of pine and salt. Afternoon sunlight slanted through the trees, gilding the pine needles that carpeted the sandy soil.

Tom unlocked the trunk. "Step right up and claim your baggage!" he said gaily.

Julia wrestled with the garage door but the lock was rusted shut. In the end, they carried the bags and boxes around to the front and went in through the porch.

Inside Julia scurried about, pulling up shades and opening the windows. Beth lingered, running fond hands over the wicker furniture and patting familiar cushions. Then she made for the stairs. On the landing, she paused outside the tiny room Dave and she had long ago dubbed The Clubhouse. Remembering marathon Monopoly sessions played out there on rainy days, she smiled reminiscently. Then she went on up to the sleeping porch. It had been Dave's chosen lair. She closed her eyes. Perhaps if she wished hard enough . . . She heard a timid step behind her. Silently she willed Grace away.

"Your mother said I could sleep here," Grace said. "But if you want to—"

"I don't care."

"No, really. You used to complain Dave always got first dibs."

"Let's share it," Beth said with a sense of release. "There's two beds."

Grace's face lit up. "Oh, yes!" she breathed. "It's going to be a terrific summer. I just know it."

After breakfast the next day, Julia said, "The rest of the unpacking can wait. Tom and I have to market. Why don't you two go to the beach?"

They needed no urging. Scrambling into bathing suits, they sprinted down the path to the water. Beth shouted, "Last one in's a rotten egg," and hurled herself off the dock. She surfaced gasping with cold. Moments later, Grace hit the water beside her. "Oh! Oh!" she squealed. "It's freezing!"

"Let's practice our surface dives," Beth said with false bravado. She put both hands over her head and arched down through the green waters. Out of the corner of her eye, she spied a crab burrowing for cover on the sandy bottom. Grabbing it behind the claws, she came up to brandish it—pincers snapping—in her friend's face.

Grace screamed and splashed for shore.

Beth's teeth were chattering. She let go of the crab and made for the beach. "Dave used to do that to me," she gasped.

Grace grinned. "Your lips are purple. Let's get dry."

They spread out their towels and lay down. Gradually the sun warmed their chilled bodies. The lapping of waves against the shore was soporific. Beth was half-asleep when a shadow darkened the glare behind her closed lids.

"Sleeping beauty," Tom mocked.

She opened her eyes and sat up. He was wearing an ancient pair of Dave's trunks. She eyed his white chest with distaste.

"Aren't you going to swim?"

"What kind of madman d'you take me for? This water's only fit for penguins and polar bears. Not middle-aged Irishmen."

"Irish, my foot!" she snapped. "You're as American as I am."

"What are you two jawing about?" Grace said sleepily. "C'mon. Let's go for a walk along the beach."

Beth trailed after them, taking care to obliterate Tom's footprints with her own.

Suddenly Tom stopped short, pointing. "What's that?"

Grace laughed. "It's a horseshoe crab, silly. Haven't you ever seen one before?"

"They don't grow on the streets of Manhattan. And I've no money for fancy seashore vacations."

Beth was tempted to retort, Yeah. And you won't get a job so's not to give your wife the money. But she kept silent. Tom was looking at her; she was sure he knew what she was thinking.

"There's another," said Grace.

"Watch this," Tom said. He fished out a length of string and pounced on the crabs. Deftly he tied their tails together, then let them go again. Released, they scuttled off in opposite directions only to be brought up short, struggling to get away.

Tom roared with laughter. Frozen with shock, the girls said nothing. After a time the silence penetrated. Tom's laughter trailed off into chuckles to die away altogether. Under the girls' accusing stare, he flushed and bent to release his victims.

"Just teasing," he muttered. "I wasn't going to hurt them. You know that, don't you?"

It was hard to sleep those first nights on the Cape. In the city the night was as noisy as day with voices, engines, squealing brakes, and horns. By now, Beth was so used to it she paid no attention. But in the country she was aware of every sound—the whirr of crickets, wind keening through the pines, the slap of waves on the shore. She imagined she could hear the flare of fireflies beyond the screens. Like bursts of flak.

Why had Tom tormented the crabs? It was cruel. Yet Tom was not a cruel man. Even through her resentment she was sure of that. It was Tom who had known how she felt that day at her mother's. Tom had been the first to point a finger at Ben's cruelty to Grace. Which was worse, then? To tease an animal or wound another human?

She slipped into sleep at last. Hours later something roused her. Heart pounding with terror, she sat up. It came again. A hoarse shout from somewhere in the house. She let out an involuntary squawk. Through the gloom she could see Grace sitting bolt upright in the other bed.

"What was that?" Grace quavered.

"I don't know."

Again the cry chilled them. This time they could distinguish words. "Don't. Oh, don't! I didn't mean it. Oh, God! They're after me." The cry rose to a shriek.

Beth hurled herself onto Grace's bed; they clung together. Grace was trembling so hard the bedsprings shook.

There were footsteps in the hall. "Don't be frightened," Julia said in a shaky whisper. "Tom had a nightmare. Something about monsters chasing him. I don't understand it. Usually he sleeps like a log."

"Maybe it's the strange bed," said Beth.

"Maybe." Her mother stifled a yawn. "It's late. We'd better get back to sleep. Good-night, girls."

Grace nudged Beth. "We know what was after him, don't we? Serves him right."

Beth did not answer. She got back into her own bed and pulled the covers up to her chin. As sleep closed over her, she heard Tom call, "Sorry, everyone. I didn't mean to scare you."

There was a hint of laughter in Julia's reply. "Aren't you glad we have a man around the house, girls?"

13

Tom stayed for two weeks. He took care of the heavy chores—mending screens, repairing the dock, putting both sailboat and mooring in the water. He even cajoled Julia's car—cranky after its winter-long captivity in a garage—back to reliable service. And he proved adept at laying fires. They took to eating supper before the hearth when blustering nor'easters turned the unheated cottage damp and draughty.

Tom never spoke of the incident on the beach. He avoided the shore altogether, apparently preferring to spend his spare time reading in the hammock on the porch. Beth wondered if it were embarrassment. Or whether, like her mother, he disliked sun and sand. As the days grew warmer, Julia swam occasionally. But she never lay down to dry on the beach, instead scurrying for cover indoors.

"I'm dark skinned enough," she would explain. "My mother used to call me 'that skinny little brown thing.' " She said it with a smile, but Beth knew she considered herself homely. Perhaps it was why she so often wore that deprecating smile that drove Beth to mingled pity and remorse. As if she herself were responsible.

They used precious gas coupons to drive Tom to Hyannis for his train. To her astonishment, Beth was sorry to see him go. He had been unfailingly helpful. And her mother was almost mellow in his company. Even Grace was more herself than she had been all year.

When they reached the station the engine was snorting fire—a dragon straining at the leash. Tom hugged Julia and turned to the girls. "Take care of her," he said. "Don't let her fret about Dave."

"We won't," Beth promised. "There's nothing to worry about yet. He's still in Alabama. He'll be safe there."

"Except from chiggers and heat stroke," he said. "Take it from me. I was a soldier once."

"A soldier!" Grace exclaimed in disbelief. "You're much too old."

"In the First World War."

Tom a soldier? Beth wanted to ask if he had seen combat; just then the train let out an ominous hiss. Tom picked up his suitcase and joined the crush of vacationers and servicemen crowding onto the coaches. He hung out the window waving as the train pulled away.

Nearby a young woman wept; the tears left streaks in her makeup. A toddler clinging to her skirts gazed anxiously up into her face. She paid no attention. She seemed to have forgotten his existence.

Beth's throat tightened. She glanced at her mother. Julia went and put a hand on the young woman's arm. A long look passed between them. Then the younger woman smiled, gulped once or twice, and bent to pick up the child. Clutching him so hard he whimpered, she walked away.

"Do you think . . ." Beth stammered. "I mean . . . I bet she was seeing her husband off for overseas."

Julia did not answer. Her face was twisted with distress.

"I'm glad Dave's still in this country," Grace announced.

"And Ray," Beth said swiftly.

Julia roused herself. "Have you heard from him?"

The question stabbed. Why didn't he write? Had he forgotten her? Or didn't he care anymore?

Julia took her hand as they walked toward the parking lot. Beth squeezed back, grateful for her understanding. Once in the car she slumped on the seat, mood as gray as the weather.

Sudden rain splattered the windshield. Julia sat motionless

behind the wheel. At last she said with an effort, "How about lunch and a movie since we're in town? It doesn't look like much of a beach day."

"Neat!" said Grace. "It'll cheer us up. I'm going to miss Tom."

It was all very well for her, Beth thought. But would she have said the same about Ben's girlfriend? Wife, she corrected herself. She couldn't seem to get used to Ben being married to Mrs. Janeway. She stole a look at Grace as they drove off, but Grace paid no attention. She was staring out the window, bouncing a little with anticipation. As the theater came into view, she cried, "Oh, look! *Now Voyager* is playing. I've seen it, but I don't mind going again. It's terrific. It has Bette Davis and Paul Henreid. Remember, Beth? He was Ingrid Bergman's husband in *Casablanca*."

"Sounds good to me," Julia murmured. "All right with you, Beth?"

She nodded absently. Paul Henreid. She had liked him. Not as much as Humphrey Bogart, of course. And no one could ever measure up to Laurence Olivier. Still . . .

They had lunch at a nearby soda fountain. The weather worsened steadily. By the time they reached the theater, the rain was pelting down. A crowd of thwarted sun worshipers milled about the ticket window.

The air inside was thick with smells of popcorn and stale butter. Beth sniffed happily. Somehow going to the movies was more of a treat here than in the city. If only Dave and Ray were with them!

The lights dimmed. A blast of martial music announced the newsreel. Beth felt her mother flinch as battle scenes—men struggling onto beaches raked by fire, and corpses washing back and forth in the surf—flashed on screen.

Grace buried her face in her hands. "I can't watch."

Beth eyed her with contempt. Proud of her own stoicism, she fixed her gaze on the scene. The dead did not shock her. They hardly seemed human. More like department store dummies. The reel shifted to the home front. Combat shots gave way to pictures of the president reviewing troops. Dockworkers cheered as his wife Eleanor christened a warship with champagne as it slid down the ways.

At last the main feature began. Beth was intrigued with the tale of a lonely spinster who emerged from treatment for a nervous breakdown to fall in love with the suave Henreid. She thrilled for the lovers as they embraced on a balcony above Rio, and ached for their plight when they could not marry because of Henreid's loyalty to his incurably ill wife. She shed tears at the fade-out line—delivered to soaring violins—"Oh, Jerry! Let's not ask for the moon. We have the stars."

Julia was silent all the way home, and over the cold supper that followed. Ominously silent. Beth's heart sank. The signs were all too familiar. But her mother wouldn't slide back into melancholy just because Tom left, would she? Or had Dave's departure finally caught up with her? Oh, Dave, Beth thought. Why aren't you here? I need you.

Grace spoke little. She kept looking to Beth. As if for answers. She said at last, "Let's go down to the beach. The rain's stopped." Her eyes were frightened.

Beth would have refused, but her mother waved them away. "Run along. I have things to do."

Not wanting to abandon her but reluctant to spy, Beth let Grace urge her down the beach path. Belated sunlight cast glittering darts across the waters as they emerged from the pine wood, but the sand was still heavy with rain. They walked out onto the dock and sat dangling their feet into the water.

"I guess the newsreel upset her," Beth ventured. "And Tom's leaving."

Grace frowned. "I think it was the movie. I feel awful that I suggested it."

"Why? It was great."

"Don't you see? Bette Davis had to go to a sanitarium. A mental hospital. It probably reminded her."

Beth shifted uneasily. She never talked of her mother's illness with Grace. "I didn't think of that," she muttered. Suddenly she was afraid. Of what she did not know; she wasn't sure she wanted to. Her heart was pounding.

"Let's go back."

Her anxiety was contagious. Grace paled beneath her tan. They scrambled up and started to run. Dusk had fallen under the trees, but no light shone from the cottage. They pushed the screen door open and dashed into the living room. At the foot of the stairs they stopped and listened. The house was quiet. Deathly quiet.

"Mom!" Beth shouted. There was no reply.

She took the steps two at a time, Grace close behind. Julia's door was open, but the room was unlit. They burst in to find her sitting by the window. She turned her head but did not speak.

"Mom," Beth said again. "What are you doing here in the dark?"

"Thinking."

"We called. Didn't you hear us?"

"I heard."

Beth looked helplessly at Grace. She took up the questioning. "Don't you feel well, Julia?"

"I'm all right. You two can go to bed." It was a dismissal.

Baffled, they turned away. It was too early for sleep. And they were unwilling to leave Julia alone upstairs. At last they stretched out on their beds and tried to read.

The house was still. A sick-room hush. Beth's legs twitched and cramped. She said a little desperately, "She'll be okay tomorrow."

"Oh, sure," Grace agreed. Too quickly.

Stunned with worry and fatigue, they fell asleep at last. In the morning Beth woke with a start. The sleeping porch was flooded with sunshine. Grace still slept. No more than the tip of her nose and a few strands of hair showed outside the bedclothes.

Beth swung her feet to the floor and tiptoed out into the hall. At the head of the stairs she hesitated, then turned toward her mother's room. To her dismay, Julia still sat in her chair fully dressed.

"Did you get up early?" Beth said. Let her say yes, she prayed. Don't let her say she stayed up all night!

"I never went to bed," Julia said tonelessly.

"Oh, Mom!" She put her arms about her and pulled her to her feet. "Come on," she implored. "Let's go downstairs. I'll make tea."

Julia came without protest. Once in the kitchen, she shouldered Beth aside and bustled about as if nothing had happened.

"Scrambled or fried?" she demanded.

"Huh?"

"How do you want your eggs?"

"Oh . . . uh, fried."

The kettle began to whistle. Beth turned off the burner and poured two cups. Julia dished up the eggs. She made no pretense of eating, only hunched at the table sipping her tea.

Beth said finally, "Was it Tom's leaving?"

Her mother's face crumpled. "No—Dave." Her voice broke on the name. She turned her face away.

"But it's been two weeks. You were okay till now."

"With Tom here I didn't have time to think. He can always make me laugh." She raised a trembling hand to her mouth.

Then with an effort she leaned over to pat Beth's cheek. "Just give me time. I'll be right as rain before you know it."

But it was weeks before she was herself. She spent much of the time alone in her room. Beth and Grace hung around The Clubhouse playing game after game of Monopoly. They took turns bicycling down to the general store for supplies. They cooked for themselves; Julia ate next to nothing. Beth never wanted to see another hot dog.

Time slowed. A record player running down. The sole reminder of the outside world was the nightly news. The girls listened religiously, turning the volume low so as not to upset Julia.

She had to be coaxed out of her clothes and into bed each night. In the morning it was all to do over. The first few evenings, Beth was embarrassed at her mother's nakedness before Grace. But as time passed, dressing and undressing her became a game. Like playing with dolls.

Every evening the girls took turns reading aloud from the collection of Dr. Fu Manchu mysteries with which some long-forgotten tenant had stocked the cottage. For some reason they amused Julia, though Beth began to have nightmares about the sinister Chinese doctor and his following of stranglers and knife throwers.

One night, during a storm, Grace woke with a wild scream and climbed into bed with her. They lay clinging together as the old house creaked and shook before onslaughts of wind and rain.

Julia revived gradually. The blankness of her face dissolved into life and laughter. The days settled back into their normal vacation rhythm.

On a sunny morning toward the end of July, Beth and Grace set off on bicycles, their picnic lunches in the baskets. It was the first time they had strayed; they pedaled with the frenzy of escaping jailbirds.

"Wait up," Grace gasped finally. "I can't go so fast."

Streaming with sweat, they pulled over onto the shoulder of the road and dismounted.

"Where are we going?" Grace panted.

"There's a deserted house on the Osterville road. I've always wanted to explore it."

"Super!" Grace agreed. "We can be French resistance fighters. Maquis. Carrying messages behind enemy lines."

Beth dropped her voice to a whisper. "We've got to be careful. Gestapo headquarters is just behind that clump of trees."

They started off again possessed by new urgency. Every so often they glanced over their shoulders, eyes peeled for signs of pursuit.

At the next turnoff, Beth signaled and swooped left. They were out of the woods now; their way lay between open fields. Heat mirages shimmered like water on the hot tar. Beth felt perilously exposed. There was no cover here, no place to hide if the Germans came upon them.

A mile or so further on she spied their destination, a weatherbeaten shack set well back from the road. She could just make out the outlines of an overgrown track leading to it. She got off the bike and pushed it along the ruts.

Suddenly she heard the roar of an approaching car. With one accord, the girls dropped their bikes and crouched low in the weeds. The car passed without slowing. They heaved a sigh of relief.

"Whew!" said Grace. "That was a close call."

"Come on," Beth urged. "But keep down." Leaving the bicycles where they had fallen, they wriggled commando fashion on their stomachs to the house. Beth stole a quick look about, then pulled herself up to peer into a window. Nothing moved inside.

She tried the door. It was warped shut. Backing off, she ran full tilt at it with her shoulder. It sprang open with a crash she was sure could be heard for miles. She froze. Then beckoning Grace to follow, she stepped over the threshold.

They found themselves in a small dim room festooned by cobwebs. The dust of years lay thick upon the floor. With each step they stirred up a cloud; particles hovered in the sunbeams filtering through the grimy windows. Strips of wallpaper stained with damp hung loose from the walls. The only furniture was a table and two chairs tilting drunkenly on buckled floorboards.

"Look!" Grace hissed. "It's set."

Beth's eyes followed the pointing finger. Sure enough, the table was set for two.

"Where'd they go?" she said in bewilderment.

Grace did not answer. Instead she tiptoed to the open door in the far wall.

Beth went to peer over her shoulder. The room beyond was as sparsely furnished as the first. Board shelves over an iron sink held a scant collection of crockery and rusted cans. The stove, black and grease encrusted, stood opposite. Nothing more.

Beth shuddered. "It's spooky," she whispered. "They must have gotten up and walked away. Right in the middle of a meal."

"Do you think the Gestapo got them?"

"Don't be silly! This isn't a game anymore. Something awful happened here." She saw Grace flush. "I'm sorry," she said. "It's just . . . well . . . There must have been a . . ." The word tragedy was on her lips. She could not bring herself to say it.

"Maybe someone got sick," Grace suggested.

"Then why would they just walk out? And why didn't they come back? No. More likely there was a fight."

"Let's go upstairs. Maybe we'll find a clue."

They started up, testing each step lest the rotting wood give way, tumbling them down into the cellar below. The second floor was stifling, an unfinished attic baked to furnace heat by sunlight beating on the tin roof. At one end stood a sagging bed-stead, at the other a broken-down chest of drawers.

Grace approached the bed cautiously, as though expecting something to leap at her. She stretched out a hand, then jerked it back.

"What is it?" Beth whispered. By now her own nerves were taut.

"Blood! There's blood on the mattress."

"There can't be."

"See for yourself."

Sure enough, a brown stain marred the filthy ticking. Beth shrugged. "Could be anything."

"You're the one that said there was a fight."

"I said 'likely.' That means there might have been one. Any-way, I meant an argument. Not a murder. It's probably rust."

"It's blood!" Grace insisted. "The ticking is stiff with it. Rust wouldn't do that."

"So how'd it get there?" As she spoke, she wondered why she bothered to argue. Did it matter what had happened? Or how? Everything about the little house bore witness to failure and loss. A wave of sadness overwhelmed her.

"I know," Grace announced. "Whoever lived here killed her-self. Right on this bed."

Beth managed to say calmly, "What about the table? How do you explain that?"

"The husband told his wife he was leaving. At dinner. And she picked up a knife, and ran upstairs, and—"

"Why didn't he stop her? Or go for help?"

"He didn't care. If he had, he wouldn't have run out on her. But she sure showed him."

Fascinated in spite of herself, Beth said, "Where did he go afterward?"

Grace's face twitched. Beth could have sworn she suppressed a giggle. "To California!"

Somewhere in the house a trapped fly buzzed. Without warning, Beth's stomach churned. She stumbled downstairs and outside to lean against the doorpost, gulping great draughts of clean sunny air. At last she picked up her bike and prepared to mount.

Grace had followed. She caught at her. "You think I'm making this up, don't you?"

"Well—"

"I'm not. I'm not! It's all there. Anyone can figure it out. It's like when Mummy and I moved out of Philadelphia. Our stuff left marks. You could tell where everything had been—the furniture, the pictures, us even. By now the people that bought the house know all about us." She brushed the hair back from her face with an angry gesture. Her fingers left grimy tracks. "I don't want people to know about me. It's humiliating. I hate it!"

She eyed Beth narrowly. "Know what's wrong with you? You don't want to talk about this. You don't even want to think about it. You figure it will go away if you don't. Well, you're wrong! Things don't just go away. Not ever." Her nails dug into Beth's arm. "I'll tell you something else. The last couple of weeks you were scared. You were afraid Julia might—"

Beth found her voice. "I don't have to listen to this!" She flung herself on the bike and bumped down the track. She thought she heard Grace call after her; she would not look back.

Julia must have been watching for them, because she was at the garage door when they wheeled in. Beth's heart missed a beat. Had something gone wrong?

But her mother was smiling. "Look, girls. Mail. A nice long letter from Dave. And one for you, Beth. I think it's from Ray."

Conscious of their stares, Beth said only, "I'll take it into the woods to read." Not waiting for an answer, she ran. Once out of sight, she slid to the ground with her back against a tree. The bark was rough through her thin polo shirt. She wriggled luxuriantly.

For a moment she hugged the letter to her, almost afraid to read. Then with trembling fingers, she tore it open. Ray's handwriting leaped out at her. "Dear Beth, I'm sorry I took so long to write. Basic training keeps you pretty busy. Reveille at five and on the go till lights out. But I'm not sorry to be here. I keep thinking of Sydney Carton in A *Tale of Two Cities*. Remember? 'It is a far far better thing that I do than I have ever done. . . .' And Thomas when he refused to hide. It's no good running away. It only makes things worse. So when the war is over . . ." Her eyes blurred. She dug her knuckles into them and sniffled. "I'll write soon again. This is just to let you know I'm alive and kicking. Also full of chigger bites and heat rash." She grinned. Tom had known what he was talking about. "Please write. I miss you and love you. Ray."

Quite suddenly the solitude she had worn like armor was gone. Because if Ray still loved her, nothing mattered so much. Nothing could hurt her. Not Grace's accusations, not Dave and Ray's absence, not her father's disapproval nor his difficulties with Jean, not even Julia's illness.

She closed her eyes. The dappled sunlight was warm on her face. She did not know how long she drowsed before she became aware of someone watching. She looked up with a start to find Grace standing over her.

"I'm sorry," Grace said. "I shouldn't have said what I did about Julia."

"You were right," Beth admitted. "I was scared."

They were silent a moment. Then Grace asked, "How's Ray?"

"Fine. How about Dave?"

"He doesn't say much. Just talks about basic training."

"Ray says he—" She blushed and burst out, "Oh, Grace! Won't it be wonderful when they come back?"

"Sure, but . . ." Grace looked wary.

"In a few years we can get married. You and Dave, and Ray and me."

"I'm never going to get married."

Beth stared. "I thought you and Dave—"

"Well, you thought wrong. Do you suppose I'd let some guy walk out on me? Like Popsie, or the guy in that house back there?"

"But that was just a story we made up. You don't know what really happened. Besides, Dave wouldn't walk out on you. And if you don't get married, you'll be all alone."

"Miss Gilles says women are better off on their own."

"Oh, Miss Gilles!" Beth said scornfully.

"What's wrong with her?"

"Nothing. Only she's an old maid. Naturally she'd say that."

"She happens to be the most exciting person I ever met," Grace flared.

"Okay, okay. Don't get sore. I'm sorry."

Grace gave a strained laugh. "So'm I. Let's not spoil the rest of the vacation fighting. I have to go to California soon." Her face tightened, then relaxed again. "Want to go for a swim? Then we won't have to take a bath tonight." She turned back to the house.

Beth followed. As she walked her hand strayed to her pocket, seeking out the letter to assure herself of its reality.

14

Robert and Jean arrived the first week of August. Julia had been in a frenzy of preparation for days. Marketing and cleaning. Even cooking. You'd think she was the housekeeper, Beth thought indignantly.

Her father was in a holiday mood; over Julia's protests that the refrigerator was full of food, he insisted on taking them out to dinner that first night.

"What have you been doing?" he teased. "Giving the local boys a run for their money?"

Beth shot Grace a warning look. She wasn't going to mention Julia's breakdown, was she?

Grace merely shrugged. "We kept busy. The same old stuff— swimming, sunbathing, sailing. As for boys—"

"I don't suppose there are many around with the war on," Jean said. "It must have been dull for you."

Beth wished they would stop harping on the war. It might set her mother off again.

Robert Michaels chuckled. "Grace will have plenty of male company on the way to California. The trains are packed with soldiers."

Julia had been silent, toying with her fried clams. Now she looked up, frowning. "Edith's going with you, isn't she?"

Grace shook her head. "I'm going by myself."

"But it's such a long trip. And it's almost impossible to find seats with all those boys on the move. Tom stood most of the way back to New York."

Beth squirmed. Why couldn't she keep her mouth shut about

Tom? Bad enough that Grace had known they shared a bedroom. She eyed her father from under her lashes; he seemed unconcerned. Still, he had known since the day they left that Tom was along.

"I can take care of myself," Grace insisted. "Besides, Mummy wouldn't be caught dead anywhere near Popsie. Or that woman." Her voice was hard.

Jean bridged the awkward pause. "You must be dying to see him. It's been months, hasn't it?"

Grace made no reply.

Julia and she were to drive back to New York the next morning. Before they left, Julia drew Beth aside. "Have a good rest, darling. A real vacation. I know what a nuisance I've been." She laughed self-consciously. "You took such good care of me. It's as if you were my mother."

Everything in Beth protested, But I'm not! You're my mother and you're supposed to take care of me. Not the other way around. All she said was, "C'n I ride down to the main road on the running board?"

As far back as she could remember it had been their summer treat. Reserved for the untraveled roads of the Cape. Dave and she would stand on opposite running boards—legs akimbo for balance—holding on for dear life as the car jounced along. Sometimes she pretended she was in the cockpit of a World War I fighter plane. Like the one Errol Flynn had piloted in *Dawn Patrol*. She had seen the movie seven times. That was before she had discovered Laurence Olivier.

The treat had lost its savor. Dave was gone. His absence felt like a hole in space. A planet wrenched from the solar system. Julia stopped at the turning to let her off. Grace stuck her head out the window. "Promise you'll forward my mail. Miss Gilles might write."

168

Beth wanted to retort, She hasn't yet. But her friend's look—half-ashamed, half-entreating—silenced her. She gave Julia a glancing peck on the cheek. Her eyes filled. Beth turned away.

As she scuffed along the sandy track back to the cottage, she kept thinking of Grace's words. Miss Gilles. Always Miss Gilles. What about Dave?

Ray had written several times. Waking at night sometimes, Beth would go to the bureau and stand there in the dark touching his letters. As if she could touch Ray himself so.

She spent long hours over her replies, writing and rewriting till her fingers were black with ink. They remained stilted and inadequate. Worse, childlike. What was there for her to write about, after all? Was she to admit that while he fought the war, Grace and she were kiting around the countryside pretending to be resistance fighters? Or that her mother . . . But, no! It was bad enough that once, testing whether he could still love her if he knew, she had confessed her mother's illness. In the past tense, of course. He wasn't to know it was still going on. Divorce, remarriage, mental illness—they were no one's business but her own. And Dave's. How she missed him! He understood.

Grace had never again asked about Ray's letters. There was no teasing, no wheedling, no offer of shared secrets. Perhaps because there were none to share. Grace did not write to Dave. She wrote to no one but Miss Gilles. Not even her mother. Edith wrote weekly, professionally typed letters on office stationery. Grace tossed them into the wastebasket unread. Finding them there unopened, Beth smuggled them out to the garbage lest Julia come upon them and worry.

As the time for her departure to California neared, Grace had closed up. Girding herself, Beth guessed. Shutting out everyone and everything as she had so often that past year.

Beth found her father on the porch steps reading the newspaper when she reached the cottage. Sunlight fell full on his head; she noticed with a pang how gray he was. Or had she forgotten?

"They get off all right?" he asked.

"Uh-huh."

"Julia looked fine. The Cape always agrees with her."

She stared. Could he really not have seen how pale and subdued her mother was? Was he blind? Or didn't he care?

"How would you like some tennis lessons this month? It will be quiet for you without Grace."

Avoiding his eyes, she nodded. She knew she should be sorry to see Grace and her mother leave. But she had been strung up for so long, braced for whatever happened. Now all she could feel was relief. A lightening. The summer stretched before her. Lazy. Peaceful.

Her father put down the paper and stretched. "Want to go swimming?"

This time she nodded with enthusiasm. She longed for the translucent waters. To sink into the dark peace of the sea.

The days ran downhill after that. It seemed no time at all before they were back in the city. Beth was happy to be home. She loved New York at this time of the year. Drowsing in the last of summer's heat, it was transformed. Momentarily a gentler, kindlier place. In the long dusk she would sit for hours by the window, allowing the music of the streets—murmurous with voices and soft laughter—to wash over her.

She made no effort to get in touch with Grace. She told herself she had no time. There was too much to do getting ready for school. But she knew it was a lame excuse. The truth was, she dreaded being caught up in her friend's troubles again.

She made herself telephone the day before school opened. Only to have the maid tell her Grace was out shopping with her mother. Grace did not return the call. Beth was hurt and not a little angry. As the hours passed, anxiety replaced her irritation. What was wrong? What had Grace found in California? How was Ben?

She chose her new pink sweater set for school the next day. Ordinarily she despised pink. It reminded her of Shirley Temple. Jean had talked her into it, saying, "It will look gorgeous with your fair hair and green eyes." She would swelter in wool at this time of year, of course. But she didn't care. She always wore something new the first day.

It was odd to get up, dress, breakfast, and set off with no Dave around. Odd but exhilarating. At long last she was on her own. Beth Michaels instead of Dave's kid sister.

It was still early when she set off for school, but she found a crowd of students waiting for the doors to open. Spying Grace, she waved.

Grace did not return the salute. Beth elbowed her way to her side.

"How was California?"

"Okay."

She looked closely at her. Grace was so tan her eyes glittered startlingly against the bronzed skin.

"You look fabulous! Did you go to the beach every day? What's the Pacific like?"

"Popsie has a pool."

"His own swimming pool?"

"Nearly everyone out there does. Especially movie stars."

"Did you meet any?"

"A few. Popsie's firm represents them. They're always getting divorced."

Beth changed the subject. "Feels funny, doesn't it?"

"What does?"

"Jefferson without Dave and Ray. Every time the phone rings, I think it's going to be Ray."

Grace looked startled. "How can he call you? He's in the army."

"You know what I mean. When you miss someone you keep looking for them. Hoping to see their face."

There was a silence. Beth rushed to fill it, repeating, "How was California? And Ben?" Until that moment she hadn't known, hadn't let herself know how much rode on the answer. She missed Ben. His absence left a gap that no one else could fill.

"Popsie's okay." Grace clamped her lips tight.

Casting about for a safer topic, Beth said, "D'you think we'll have Miss Gilles again for homeroom?"

Grace's face tightened. "She's not coming back."

"Not coming back? Why?"

"She's going to be principal of a girls' school in Connecticut. I had a letter."

"She didn't say anything about it last spring."

"She didn't know. It came up over the summer."

The magnitude of the disaster left Beth speechless. Just then the doors opened. They pushed inside and started up the stairs. When they reached their homeroom, Grace took a letter from her purse. She handed it to Beth without comment.

In Miss Gilles's spiky hand—familiar from countless acid comments on English papers—Beth read.

"My dear Grace,

"I have put off writing. For that I owe you an apology. But by now I am sure the summer away has given you perspective on a difficult year. So it will not come as too much of a blow to learn that I shall not be returning to Jefferson. This summer I was offered and accepted the post of principal at a fine girls' academy in Connecticut. I deeply regret this interruption of our association. But distance need not spell an end to friendship. We can still exchange letters and visits. Please do continue sending your stories and poems. I shall be only too happy to read and comment on them. You have a bright future before you, I know. Have a good year and keep in touch.

"Yours, Eloise Gilles."

Eloise. Beth hadn't known her name was Eloise. It was too soft. Too feminine. It jarred somehow.

She looked up to meet Grace's eyes. They were fixed on her with such intensity she dropped her own. "It's a nice letter," she faltered. "She says she wants to hear from you. And she's sorry."

"Sorry!" Before the scorn in Grace's voice, Beth felt herself redden. "Sorry! I thought she was my friend. I trusted her. I went to her when there was no one else. And she has the nerve to talk about perspective! Does she think I can forget what's happened? Doesn't she know what it was like out there with Popsie and that woman and her kids? I wrote to her. Didn't she read my letters? Oh, what's the use?" Her voice was shrill. About them students fell silent.

Beth touched her arm, but Grace shook her off. At that instant the bell rang and a short, gray-haired woman came into the room.

"Good morning, class," she said. "I'm Mrs. Johnson, your new homeroom and English teacher. I should like to start off by having you introduce yourselves. The dark-haired girl in the front row may begin." She nodded at Grace.

Moments passed, but Grace did not reply. Beth glanced nervously at her. Her face betrayed nothing. The silence drew out. In the hush, Beth was aware of every movement, every rustle, every breath. Someone in a back row coughed. Beth started.

The teacher repeated, "The dark-haired girl in the front row may begin!" There was an edge to the words.

Still Grace did not speak. Hoping to jar her into response, Beth said as loudly as she dared, "I'm Beth Michaels." Grace remained mute.

Beth could bear it no longer. She said rapidly, "Her name is Grace Abbot, and I don't think she feels well. Can I take her to the nurse's office?"

Mrs. Johnson smiled frostily. "Of course, Beth. But hurry back. Our homeroom is scheduled to go to the bookstore at ten. If Grace is not better by then, you may pick up her books for her."

Beth grabbed Grace's arm. She came without resistance. When the door closed behind them, Beth burst out, "What's wrong with you? Do you want to get yourself in dutch the first day?"

Grace shrugged. "I don't care. Why should you?"

"I'm your best friend, that's why."

"Are you? I thought Miss Gilles was my friend, too. She left me."

The flat voice reminded Beth of her mother. Brushing the comparison aside, she said, "Well, are you coming?"

"Where?"

"To the nurse's office."

Grace shook her head. "I'm okay." She turned back to the classroom without a word of thanks. Nothing for it but to follow.

For Beth, the annual expedition to the bookstore was a high point of the school year. Holding her new texts for the first time, it seemed to her the wisdom of the ages was within her grasp. An intoxicating promise of initiation and power. Each year she set herself impossible schedules for mastery. Each year she fell short. It made no difference. Each year she sallied forth to buy books with the same thrill of excitement.

As they walked down the street to the store, she kept stealing glances at Grace. At last she ventured, "Why wouldn't you tell Mrs. Johnson your name? It was rude."

"So what?"

"Don't you want her to like you?"

"I don't give a damn if she likes me or not!" Grace snapped. "I wanted Miss Gilles to like me. So I was as nice and polite as I knew how. Look where it got me. She's gone. And remember when I stayed with you last winter? I helped every way I could. It didn't make you like me better. It just made you mad. You couldn't wait to get rid of me."

Beth would have protested, but Grace rushed on. She was hurling words like weapons. Bitter, wounding words. "It's true! I'm not blind. I know what I saw. And don't think I don't know what people think of Mummy either. That she's awful to be so angry. To say the things she does. Well, you know what? She'd be nuts to act nice after she's been treated so badly!"

"But I didn't mean . . ." Beth faltered. "I mean . . . I just didn't want to see you get hurt. Well, you know the kind of things she says about Ben. And I know how much you love him, so . . ." Grace's mouth opened, but Beth hurried on, "Anyway, promise you won't do anything dumb. Like talking back, or not getting your work done, or—"

"Oh, mind your own business!" Grace shouted.

Beth began to tremble. A deep internal quaking she was powerless to control. To her dismay, she felt the corners of her mouth turn up in an involuntary half smile. She dropped back to walk by herself.

She made a show of enthusiasm at the bookstore. But it had gone flat. The new books were just that. Books. No longer keys to an exalted world. All the way back to school she kept fingering them, hoping against hope to recapture the lost enchantment.

The rest of the day passed in familiar routines—class schedules, course outlines, locker assignments. She went about them mechanically, avoiding Grace's angry glare.

At day's end she fled. For once, her father was home before her.

"What're you doing home so early?"

"Dave's coming. He has embarkation leave."

"You mean . . ."

He nodded grimly. "He's going overseas."

"He's only been in the army since June. And the war's almost over. Italy surrendered."

"Italy was a sideshow. The Germans are fighting for their lives. They know it's their last chance."

"When'll he be here?"

"Any minute. He called from the bus station."

"So soon?" she cried. "Why didn't you say so? I've got to clean up."

She made for the bathroom. She was splashing water on her face when a thought struck her. Still dripping, she called downstairs, "Does Mom know?"

"She's on her way. Jean asked her to dinner."

She had barely applied fresh lipstick and powder when the doorbell rang. Racing downstairs she flung herself on Dave, but Robert and Jean were before her. They stood in a tight scrimmage all hugging, laughing, and talking at once.

Beth was the first to extricate herself. She drew back and stared at her brother. In his rumpled khaki he was taller and thinner than she remembered; his hair had been shaved like an Indian brave's. But the look in his eyes—half-ironic, half-sad—was as it had been.

"You hugged us!" she said in wonder.

"I missed you all. It's great to be home." He looked around. "Where's Mom?"

"She's coming," Jean said. "Let's go down to the kitchen. We can talk while I get dinner."

It was like the old days. Yet not quite. Beth puzzled over it. What had changed? Was it Dave? Or the rest of them—her father, hanging on Dave's every word; Jean, with one eye for the dinner, one for her stepson; or her mother, flushed as if to greet a lover? Or was it Beth herself, borne up on a never to be repeated joy? In the end she gave it up. There were moments that did not bear examination. Bubbles that might burst at a touch, a breath, a thought.

"It's only spaghetti," Jean said apologetically. "It makes the meat coupons go further. If I'd known you were coming I'd have wangled a steak. Or died in the attempt."

Dave grinned. "So long as it's not Spam."

There was ice cream for dessert. Again Jean apologized. "I would have baked . . ."

Robert Michaels made an impatient sound. Jean reddened. Julia glanced at her, then looked away again. Beth thought she caught the gleam of sympathy, but her mother's face was expressionless.

Dave took out a pack of cigarettes. Beth looked apprehensively at her father. He hesitated, then lit a match and held it out. Dave leaned forward to accept the light. And with a stab of pain, Beth knew what had changed. Her brother had grown up. The Dave she knew would not come home again.

"Tell us about basic training," Jean urged.

"Nothing much to tell. Just a lot of drill and marches." He paused. "Of course, there are VD lectures. Ever hear of 'blue balls?' "

Beth snickered. She saw her father suppress a smile.

"Dave!" Jean chided. "It's lucky Grandma Michaels isn't here."

"Where are they sending you?" said Julia.

A hush fell. Beth hunched as if before an icy blast.

"I'll have an East Coast APO. That's all I can tell you."

"APO?" Beth heard herself say.

"Army Post Office. They forward overseas mail."

"So it's Europe," Julia said flatly. She drew a long breath and stood up. "I must get home. Thank you for having me, Jean."

"I'll come see you tomorrow," said Dave.

She nodded and tucked her pocketbook under her arm. The gesture caught at Beth. The rest of them were together. Only her mother had to go into the night alone. Suddenly she hated her father.

After she had gone, Dave said, "Think I'll call Grace."

It took Beth unawares. "I'm not sure . . ." she stammered.

"Is something wrong?"

"Oh, no." How could she tell him Grace would not come? Not after today.

But to her surprise, Grace agreed. Dave went to pick her up. When they got back, they came into the kitchen arm in arm. Grace greeted Beth as if nothing had happened.

"Have you heard from Ray?" Dave asked.

"I got several letters while we were at the Cape."

"Remember how upset you were about our being in separate outfits?"

"I don't know why. It doesn't seem to matter now. I'm just glad—" She broke off, appalled at what she had almost said. That she was grateful it was Dave, not Ray, who was to be sent overseas.

Misreading the hesitation, Grace put a hand on her shoulder. "He'll be all right, Beth. I'm sure of it."

A lump came into her throat. "Thanks!"

They smiled. They might never have fought at all.

"Guess I'll go up and start my homework," Beth said. "You two probably want to be alone."

"Thanks, squirt." The approval in Dave's voice warmed her.

But later, hearing them come up and close her brother's door, she had to repress a pang. She fixed her eyes on the new books, pristine in their colorful bindings. Excitement twinged. Latin. Biology. Geometry. History. French. One day, perhaps, she would be another Eve Curie. Or a classicist. Or linguist. Perhaps a historian. She grinned suddenly. Because in her wildest dreams, she couldn't imagine herself a mathematician. She was deep in Cicero when the others reappeared.

Grace was flushed. Her hair was tangled and her blouse had come untucked. She gazed adoringly at Dave.

Remembering the pressure of Ray's lips on hers, Beth trembled.

"I'm taking Grace home," Dave told her.

"I'll wait up for you."

She heard them start downstairs. A moment later there was a patter of footsteps and Grace was beside her again. "You were right," she whispered. "About everything. Dave is here for me. You, too. Not like"—she faltered and recovered—"not like Miss Gilles."

"You coming, Grace?" Dave called.

"I'll be right with you." She hugged Beth and was gone.

For months Beth had spun visions of her best friend and her brother. Why was she uneasy now? Was it jealousy?

Switching off the light, she went to sit at the window waiting for Dave to return.

15

In fifth grade they had made maps for geography, coloring in the states and capitals, and gluing on bits of cotton, metal, wood, and even coal to illustrate the products. Beth thought if she drew a time line for the fall of 1944, she would highlight the days of Dave's leave with Christmas tinsel. Shiny with happiness.

Grace came home from school with her each day; the three of them walked for hours in the park. The weather was sunny but cool. Already fall was in the air. Touches of scarlet and gold punctuated the greenery. Beth felt giddy, as though living at a great altitude. She almost burst with pride over her tall brother in uniform, with his ribbons and patches. "Fruit salad," he called them, making light of the display. But he walked with head held high and shoulders back. Quite unlike his former adolescent shamble.

Beth begged spare patches from him and sewed them to her jacket. Thus adorned, she eyed passing civilians with a sympathy bordering on scorn. They were missing out on the greatest adventure of all time. For her parents' fears she felt scant compassion. What was danger when there was a world to conquer? A world of heroism and great deeds.

She laced her talk with Dave's new vocabulary. Tossing off *sad sack* and *snafu*, *squad* and *platoon* as if she'd known and used them all her life. One day in the cafeteria she regaled her friends with *blue balls*. Though secretly she found the term repulsive. Reminiscent of those livid technicolor rumps on monkeys in the zoo.

Only Ray's silence marred her joy. She had heard no more

from him since coming back from the Cape. Could he have been shipped out without her knowing?

And then, as suddenly as it had begun, the halcyon time was over. Dave was gone. For how long no one knew. Perhaps forever.

In the weeks that followed she pored over the news, all the while wondering where her brother was. The advance of Patton's Third Army filled her with exultation, the British disaster at Arnhem plunged her into despair. In mid-October, Mrs. Johnson announced to the homeroom, "The Allies have taken Athens." Her voice trembled with emotion. Beth had a sudden vision of her brother storming the Parthenon. The crumbling temple whose picture had hung in every classroom she could remember. She had to smile at herself. Because not two days before, she had pictured Dave in the thick of fighting on the western front. If only they would hear from him!

As time passed she began to worry about her father, too. It was disconcerting. He had always seemed so strong, so self-sufficient. Forbiddingly so. She had expected her mother to buckle under the strain. But Julia maintained a precarious calm. It was Robert Michaels who grew grayer and more fine drawn daily. The circles under his eyes were like bruises.

His hours were longer than ever. He was rarely home before eight or nine o'clock, only to grab a hasty dinner and go out again to a meeting of the refugee committee. Jean made no open complaint, but at night Beth would hear raised voices from their bedroom. As if that weren't enough, her father had become an almost weekly commuter to Washington, often standing the whole way on troop-jammed trains.

Studying late one night, Beth wandered down to the kitchen for a snack. She found her father slumped at the table, head in his hands.

"Dad!" she cried, panicky because he was so still. "Dad!"

He opened his eyes. They were dazed with sleep at first. Then he smiled. "I must have dropped off. What time is it?"

"Almost twelve."

He yawned and ran his fingers through his hair. The gesture reminded Beth poignantly of Dave. "No sense trying to work anymore tonight. Is Jean in bed?"

"Uh-huh. She was late home from class. I had supper by myself." She could not keep the grievance from her tone.

He scowled. "I didn't want her to go back to work in the first place. The least she could do is arrange her schedule to spend more time with you. She knows how hard I'm working."

"Do you have to, Dad? We have enough money, don't we?"

"It's not just my practice. Though that's pretty frantic. It's this nightmare in Europe. It haunts me. If I could save even a few Jews . . . I've tried so hard!"

"I used to think you didn't care about things like that."

"Like what?" he said sharply.

"You know. Religion."

"It has nothing to do with religion. These are people dying. For no reason. Think of it—men, women, and children dragged from their homes and slaughtered like animals."

"Can't the government do something?"

"That's why I go to Washington so often. There have been opportunities to ransom people. Even suggestions to bomb the camps. But—" He broke off.

"Is Mr. Siegel on the committee with you?"

"Who?"

"Ray's father."

"Oh. That Mr. Siegel." He seemed to choose his words with care. "He's active with another group. We don't see eye to eye. His people insist the refugees must go to Palestine. That a Jewish homeland is the only permanent solution."

182

"What does Roosevelt say?" Again she thrilled with pride that her father knew the president.

His face darkened. "He says we must win the war first."

"Don't you agree with him?"

"There won't be any Jews left in Europe by the time we win. We have to act now if we're to save any." He got to his feet and started across the kitchen, walking stiffly like an old man.

Fear clutched her. She blurted out, "Jean says we never see you anymore." She regretted the words the moment they were spoken. They were sure to make trouble. She stammered, "I mean, we're your family. I know it's awful about the Jews, but . . . well, sometimes you seem to worry more about them than Dave!"

He turned on her a look so bleak, she shrank. In a voice of ice, he said, "My family is an extension of myself. I'm no harder on you than on myself. You'd better get used to that. All of you. As for David, you know nothing of how I feel. Nothing at all!" He reached for the light switch. The kitchen went dark.

She was frozen, unable to reply. At last she crept up to bed. It was long before she slept.

When she got home from school the next day, Jean called down, "Beth? Come up here. I want to talk to you."

Inwardly she groaned. With lagging steps she went up to the library and stuck her head in. "What's up?"

"What on earth got into you last night?"

"How do you mean?"

"I mean, when I've got a gripe with your father I'll handle it myself. I don't need you to speak for me. It seems you told him I was complaining about how hard he worked. I didn't think you'd carry tales."

"I wasn't!" Beth protested. "I just thought . . . Oh, what's the use? You wouldn't understand." How could she explain her terror and resentment? Fear her father might give way, plunging them all into the abyss. Resentment at his neglect. It was not for Jean she had spoken, but herself. She had only borrowed her stepmother's words, hoping he might listen more readily to his wife's complaints than her own. All she had done was to make it worse. She might have known.

Jean said more gently, "I almost forgot. You had a call."

"From who?"

"He didn't say. It sounded like Ray."

Beth could feel the heat rise in her face. "Is he going to call back?"

There was a twinkle in Jean's eyes. "I expect so." She paused, then went on, "I'm sorry I got mad. I know you didn't mean any harm. But with your father's temper . . ." She shook her head.

"It'll be okay, won't it? I mean, he'll get over it. He always does." She waited in vain for reassurance. Finally she retreated to her room.

The telephone rang as she was trying to study. Dropping the book, she shot into the hall, shouting, "I'll get it!" But when she picked up the receiver she could scarcely get the words out. What if it weren't Ray after all? "H'llo?" she croaked.

"Beth? It's me. Ray."

She steadied her voice. "Where are you?" She heard him chuckle. Her knees went weak.

"Home, of course. I only have a couple of days. Can you come out tonight?"

"Sure," she said with more confidence than she felt. What would her father say? It was a school night. But it was her last chance to see Ray before he went overseas.

"I'll pick you up in a little while." He hung up.

She tore back to her room. Leaving her school clothes where she stepped out of them, she pulled on stockings. In her haste her nails snagged the flimsy fabric. She swore and took out her new beige suit and put it on, peering anxiously in the mirror. Did it make her look too fat? The skirt was the narrowest she had ever worn. If only she had Grace's slim hips.

She had just finished her period; there were two pimples on her chin. They seemed prominent as twin mountain peaks. She applied makeup, slipped her feet into pumps, and teetered downstairs.

Her father met her in the hall. "You're all dressed up," he said. "Where are you going?"

"Ray's home. He asked me out."

"You know the rules. No dates on a school night."

"Let her go, Robert," Jean said from behind her. "Just this once. There's a war on."

He laughed without mirth. "I know that. Sometimes I think I'm the only one in this house who does." He turned back to Beth. "Have you finished your homework?"

She nodded dumbly. It seemed less of a lie if she kept silent.

He looked suspicious, but all he said was, "You've got too much makeup on."

Her hand flew to her chin. Flushing, she let it drop again.

"Robert!" Jean exclaimed. Her eyes met Beth's; the look was pitying. Momentarily they were allies.

The bell rang. Beth opened the door to find Ray smiling down at her. She stared hungrily at him.

"You look terrific!" he said.

"So do you."

"It's good to see you, Ray," her father said. "Is this your embarkation leave?"

Ray nodded. "Not a very long one, I'm afraid. We ship out—" He stopped.

"That's right. Don't say any more than you have to. You know the slogan, 'Loose lips can sink ships.'"

"Is Dave overseas?"

Robert Michaels's face clouded. "Yes. But as yet we've heard nothing from him."

"They say it takes time for mail to catch up."

"Are you in an infantry outfit, Ray?"

"Yes, sir. Uh . . . Beth and I had better go. My folks expect us for dinner."

Robert Michaels looked relieved. "Give them my best. And don't be too late. Beth has school tomorrow."

She struggled to swallow her disappointment. She had wanted Ray to herself. Not to share with his parents.

He took her arm as they walked toward the subway. She trembled at his touch and tried to think of something to say. He, too, seemed tongue-tied. The racket of the train was a relief, making conversation unnecessary.

As they emerged at Fourteenth Street, he said, "I missed you. I've been keeping your letters in my pocket. That way, I can take them out and look at them when I get lonely. It's almost like having you there."

With that her shyness fell away. She flung her arms around him. In the back of her mind she heard her father say, "You don't display your feelings in public. It makes people uncomfortable." She ignored it. Ray was going away to war. She might never see him again.

They clung to each other. Passersby eddied about them. Ray whispered at last, "We'd better go. Mom'll skin us alive if we spoil her dinner. She's been in the kitchen all day."

"Is she a good cook?"

"Wait till you taste her chicken and pot roast."

"Chicken and pot roast both? Who else is coming?"

"Just the four of us." He laughed at her surprise. "You don't know my mom. She thinks the army starves me. She's determined to fill me up for the duration. Didn't yours when Dave had embarkation leave?"

She was defensive. "She's not much of a cook. Anyway, it was Jean that made dinner. Not Mom." She brightened. "But she apologized for not having steak."

His hand tightened on hers. "We're having a real Shabbas meal. Except it's Wednesday. And without the challah."

"Challah?" She stumbled over the gutteral.

"You don't know anything about being Jewish, do you?" His smile robbed the words of sting. "Challah is the special Shabbas bread. Mom bakes it every Friday."

Two blocks further on, they turned in at a drab apartment building. Beth's heart beat fast as they went up in the elevator. Would the Siegels still like her? She hadn't seen them since graduation, though she had promised to visit. Would they be angry at her neglect?

Ruth Siegel flung open the door before Ray could get his key out. She drew Beth into her arms. "I'm so happy you've come!" she cried. "My Raymond will have happy memories to take away with him."

Ray's father greeted her more quietly, extending his hand with a warm "As lovely as ever, I see."

With that she forgot her doubts. The apartment was fragrant with cooking smells. Beth's mouth watered. Ruth Siegel hurried them to a small dining table set up at one end of the living room.

Beth looked about. The room was small and cramped, overful of heavy furniture. But the armchairs looked inviting. And the walls were lined with bookshelves. She thought she could identify titles in French, German, English, Russian, and Hebrew. She eyed the Siegels with new respect.

Mrs. Siegel bustled into the kitchen to reappear with platters of steaming food.

"Don't give me too much," Beth pleaded.

"A young girl needs her food. Look! It's lovely chicken and

brisket. I've been saving meat coupons. And there's salad. Nothing to that but vitamins."

Ray slanted a grin at her. "Better eat up. Or you'll never hear the end of it. You can diet tomorrow."

"Enough, Ruthie," his father cautioned. "It's Ray that's going away. Not Beth. And you can see her mother takes good care of her."

Desolation as sharp as it was unexpected swept her. Did her mother take care of her? She said hastily, "Did you know Miss Gilles is gone, Ray?"

"Where'd she go?"

"They made her principal of a girls' school in Connecticut."

"That's tough on Grace."

"It was at first. I think she's getting used to it now."

"Grace?" Mrs. Siegel inquired.

"Beth's best friend from Philadelphia. I told you about her. She moved here last year when her parents got divorced."

"This Miss Gilles was a special friend of hers?"

Beth nodded.

"Poor child. To lose her family and friend in the same year!"

At the compassion in her voice, tears came to Beth's eyes. She blinked them back.

Mr. Siegel said, "I've seen something of your father lately. At meetings. He's a fighter. A fine man. You must be very proud of him."

Beth went hot with shame. People were always telling her how lucky she was to have Robert Michaels for a father. What was wrong with her? Why couldn't she get along with him?

"No one wants to listen!" Mr. Siegel said bitterly. "By the time they do, it will be too late." His face twisted.

Ray put a hand on his. "That's why we're fighting, Dad."

"You mean you're fighting. They have no use for me. I'm an

old man. Fit for nothing but talk. Talk! While our people die."

"My father wishes he could fight, too," Beth told him. "So do I."

"Now that's enough about the war!" Ruth Siegel burst out. "Eat, everyone. Your supper's getting cold."

Over dessert, Ray returned to the subject. "You shouldn't talk like that, Dad. There's going to be a Jewish homeland in Palestine after the war. Thanks to you and your friends. And if—" He caught himself. "When I come back, I'm going to live there. They'll need people like me."

"Raymond!" Dismay was plain on his mother's face. "What about college? I've dreamed of your being a doctor."

"I'll go to the Hebrew University."

"But it's so far away."

"You want to live there?" Beth said unbelievingly.

"Don't you see? There won't be a Jewish homeland unless Jews are willing to go. Not just refugees either."

"You're American."

"I'm also a Jew."

"Let's not argue," Ruth Siegel implored. "We have so little time. Tonight let's just enjoy each other. Be happy together."

Ray opened his mouth to protest, then closed it again. He stood up. "You two sit and have your tea. Beth and I will do the dishes."

She followed him out to the tiny kitchen. She took off her jacket and hung it over the back of the step stool. Then she filled the sink with suds and piled the dishes in. She could feel Ray's eyes on her, but she would not meet the look.

His arms came round her from behind. Dropping his chin in her hair, he said, "Are you mad? I didn't mean to break it like that."

She shook her head.

"I meant for you to come with me, Beth."

"You mean leave my family and everything?"

"We'll be pioneers. Join a collective farm, a kibbutz. Oh, Beth, it will be a whole new way of life. A new kind of Jew."

For a moment she could see it. The farms, the fields, and watchtowers. Men, women, and children working together for a golden future.

She shook it off. "I don't know, Ray. I always thought I'd live here in New York. With you, of course. Dave and Grace, too. Bring up our kids here and send them to Jefferson like us."

"I don't want to live like that. It's meaningless."

She groped for something. Anything to lure him back. "What about your acting?"

"It'll have to wait. Besides, they have theater in Palestine."

She took a deep breath. Her eyes were watering. She dug her knuckles in them. The soap burned and she turned on him. "Now look what you made me do!"

For answer he swung her about and kissed her. She clung to him helplessly. "Oh, Ray! Promise you'll come home safe."

His tongue parted her lips. Her breath quickened.

"I brought the rest of the dishes," said Mr. Siegel from the door.

Beth's face flamed. She ran shaking fingers through her hair. But she could feel Ray's lips still, the hard pressure of his body. Deep inside her something fluttered. Throughout the evening the sensation kept coming back. It was like being seasick. Yet oddly thrilling. Secretly she hugged it to her.

A sliver of light still showed under the living room blinds when Ray took her home.

"D'you want to come in?" Beth said dubiously. If her father and Jean were up, they would ask Ray in to talk. It would spoil things. She did not want to remember him here; she wanted to think of him in the book-lined apartment with his parents. A real home. Though if Robert and Jean were asleep, she could smuggle him up to her room. They would lie on her bed and he would kiss her. Again she felt the tremor in her stomach.

"I'd better not," he said. "You have school tomorrow and my folks will be waiting up."

He brushed her lips with his. Then he ran down the steps and disappeared into the dark.

President Roosevelt was elected to a fourth term in November. Republicans muttered about dictatorship. But Beth's friends shared her incredulity that anyone would vote against the only president they had known. Who else was there to lead them to victory?

They heard from Dave at last. On reaching France, he had been hospitalized with flu. From there he had volunteered for a Ranger battalion.

Beth overheard her father say, "The casualties must be terrible if they're recruiting in hospitals." He sounded upset, but she glowed with pride. Rangers were like British Commandos. If only she could volunteer, too! It wasn't fair. Just because she was a girl.

And suddenly it was Thanksgiving again. In honor of the holiday they were to eat upstairs in the dining room. Beth helped Jean put the extra leaves in the table.

"Can we use the good china?" she pleaded.

Jean nodded and she clattered down to the pantry to load the flowered dishes on the dumbwaiter. She handled them reverently. Hearing her father's step, she moved to block his view. He disapproved of Jean's party china, as he did of Grandma Michaels's Passover plates. She hoped he wouldn't spoil the treat with his displeasure.

He was smiling. "Smells good, doesn't it? That bird must be

almost ready to carve. I can't wait. Jean made her chestnut stuffing."

She smiled back in relief and said, "Get the soup plates off the top shelf, will you? Jean said to leave them on the kitchen table. She wants to fill them down here."

"If you say so. I'm afraid the dumbwaiter will be awash in soup." He grinned ruefully. "They certainly didn't build these brownstones for convenience."

The doorbell rang. "I'll go," Beth offered. "It's probably Grace and Edith."

But when she opened the door, a Western Union man stood there. "Telegram, miss. For Robert Michaels. Sign here."

She scribbled her name and shut the door, wondering who would send her father a wire on Thanksgiving. She hoped it wasn't the refugee committee. It was sure to spoil the day.

"Give it to me," her father said behind her. She turned with a start. She had not heard him follow. His face had a greenish tinge in the lamplight.

"Dad! Are you okay?"

He grabbed the envelope out of her hands and ripped it open. Reading the message, he stumbled to the dining room door. "Jean!" he called in a choked voice.

Beth went cold. "Is something wrong?" Then she knew! "It's not Dave, is it?" she faltered.

Jean appeared. She read the telegram and paled. But her voice was steady. "Only missing in action, thank God! There's still a chance he's safe." She put her arms around her husband.

Tears streamed down his face; he whimpered deep in his throat. The sounds terrified Beth. He held out his hand. She longed to go to him. Instead she fled upstairs, muttering incoherently.

She slammed the door and stood against it, gasping as if

winded. Her eyes traced and retraced the room—noting the missing drawer pull on the bureau, the dents and scars on the desktop, the stain where she had spilled ink on the spread doing her homework in bed. Jean had been furious.

She was shivering. She burrowed under the bedclothes. She had a queer sense of being two distinct creatures—a wounded animal gone to ground, and an observer standing clear outside. Some show, the observer mocked. But couldn't you work up a tear or two? Even your father cried. Agonized, she retorted, I can't. I just can't cry. I wish I could!

Later Grace came. She hovered in the doorway, apparently reluctant to enter the room. Uncertain what to say or do. She was deathly pale.

The house was full of people when they came downstairs. Beth never knew where they came from. She did not understand what was said to her. Words buzzed meaninglessly in her ears. There were tearful embraces. Everyone seemed to want to hug and cry over her. Politely but firmly she repulsed them.

She drifted into the dining room. Someone had rescued dinner before it was incinerated. It appeared on the table buffet style, flanked by mismatched plates and cutlery. As though whoever chose them did not know where things were kept. Beth felt a pang for the flowered china. Then guilt overwhelmed her. Her brother was missing in action. Perhaps dead. And she was fussing over china.

Someone tapped her on the shoulder. Her heart jumped. She turned to see Bert Wasserman, a partner in her father's firm. "Take care of him," he urged.

"Who?" she whispered. Could he mean Dave? But Dave was . . .

"Robert. He needs you. He'll never ask for help, or admit what this costs him. But he feels things so deeply. Of course, you know that better than I." He sighed. "Whenever there's a moral issue at the firm, we all turn to him. He's such a good man!"

She could not bear to listen; she shrank from him.

At some point Robert and Jean went to break the news to Julia and bring her back with them. Beth retreated. As if the marks of suffering on Julia's face were badges of shame. Like the Scarlet Letter.

As the day wore on, she grew increasingly hurt and baffled at Grace. She and Edith seemed inseparable, roosting together on the piano bench like sparrows. Watching, Beth was startled by their resemblance. Angry and embittered both. Yet, for once, Edith was almost animated. Her voice boomed out above the others in the room. When she went to refresh her drink, Beth took advantage of her absence to sit beside Grace. She felt her edge away. Glancing sideways, she surprised a look of—was it anger?—on her friend's face.

"Missing doesn't mean . . . He could be a prisoner . . ." she faltered.

Grace laughed. The sound was shocking. "You don't really believe that, do you?"

"Don't you want him to be found?"

Just for a moment Grace seemed at a loss. Then she recovered herself. "I don't like to see you get your hopes up. You shouldn't care so much about people. Not Dave. Not Ray. Not anyone. Sooner or later they all let you down. Like Miss Gilles."

"But you love Dave. You said he was here for you."

"And he went away."

"He couldn't help it. There's a war on."

"People always have some excuse. But they leave you just the same. So what's the point of caring?" She got up. "I have to go find Mummy. See you in school Monday."

It's not fair, Beth thought. Last year I stuck with her. Now I need someone, and she doesn't care. Care. The word stabbed. Grace had told her not to care so much. Was she right, then? It hurt to care. Only if you didn't, what was the point of anything?

The smoke stung her eyes. She rubbed them, hoping no one would imagine she was crying and come to slobber over her. Across the room a knot of people parted to let two newcomers through. Suddenly she recognized the Siegels.

They saw her at the same instant. Ruth Siegel rushed to smother her in an embrace. She did not pull away. Her arms were comforting. Like Ray's.

"How did you know?" she whispered.

"Avram had a call from someone on the refugee committee. We came as fast as we could."

Mr. Siegel patted Beth's hand. "Men get cut off. Your brother may be a prisoner. Missing in action is no death sentence these days."

It was the comfort Jean had offered; Beth herself had passed it on to Grace. Unable to speak, she nodded. She looked up to see Jean and her parents approaching. Had they seen Ruth Siegel's hug? Were they hurt that she sought consolation elsewhere?

To her amazement, Ruth Siegel embraced her father. Comforting him like a child. Then she hugged Jean and Julia. The men drew apart, talking quietly.

At last Mr. Siegel sighed. "Come, Ruthie. We must let these people get some rest." He put a hand on Robert Michaels's arm. "Try not to worry. There's always hope."

"I know," Robert Michaels said. He tried to smile.

Beth caught at Mrs. Siegel. "Have you heard from Ray?"

"Not yet. We'll let you know as soon as we do."

Her father had recovered his composure. "Thank you for coming. It means a great deal to us. Especially Beth. You've been so kind to her."

"She's a fine girl," said Mrs. Siegel. "You should be proud of her." Turning to Jean, she added, "I left a cake on the table. So you'll have something sweet to serve." She kissed Julia. "Your David will come home safe. You'll see."

The room emptied swiftly. Presently only the Michaels family remained. Robert Michaels said, "I'll drive you home, Julia. Is there someone you'd like to call first? I'm sure Edith would come. You shouldn't be alone."

Beth heard herself say, "I'll take Mom home and stay." She looked anxiously at her father. "It's okay, isn't it? You have Jean." She could not bear to think of her mother with only Edith for company. Or even Tom.

A sudden smile lit Robert Michaels's face. But all he said was, "That's my Bethie!"

16

Going back to school felt odd. Disorienting. Because nothing had changed. Everything was just as it had been. As usual Beth's alarm went off at six forty-five. And as usual she staggered out of bed trembling at the shattering of oblivion.

She stared at herself in the mirror as she dressed, searching for some outward sign of the catastrophe. Apart from pallor and the hint of circles under her eyes, she looked exactly as she had before the telegram.

There was oatmeal for breakfast as usual. She dumped half a box of brown sugar over it and drowned the mess in cream. Her father emerged from behind his *Times* to say, "Do you have to use all that stuff? Try it plain for once. It's delicious." She paid no attention. She had heard it all before. She wondered why he bothered with the paper. Dave was no longer a participant in those far-off battles.

She piled the dishes in the sink, gave her father a hasty kiss, and banged out of the house. All the way to school, she rehearsed what she would say to friends and teachers. "Dave's missing." Or "My brother's missing in action." The words evoked no more than a dull ache. More a reverberation—like distant thunder—than true pain. And from so far off she could scarcely identify the source.

She wasn't sure if she was disappointed or relieved to find the school unchanged. She scuttled upstairs, stowed her gear, and edged into homeroom, suddenly too self-conscious to speak to anyone. Mrs. Johnson was at the board. When Beth came in, she dropped the chalk and hurried to her. Beth flipped up the desktop and pretended to search inside, hoping the teacher would not say anything.

Eyes moist with sympathy, Mrs. Johnson murmured, "I'm so sorry, Beth. I pray he'll be found safe."

A lump came into Beth's throat. She dropped her eyes. When she looked up again, the teacher had retreated to the blackboard. Students passed. Beth thought they avoided looking at her. Grace dropped a small box on her desk.

"What is it?" Beth mouthed.

"Open it and see," Grace whispered back.

Nested inside was Ben's charm on its chain. Startled, Beth looked up to surprise a strange expression on her friend's face. Something very like defiance.

All through English, Beth fingered the trinket. Did Grace mean her to keep it? What would Ben think when he found she had given it away?

There was no opportunity for questions. At the end of the period, Grace was up and out the door before Beth could move. Pulling herself together she ran after her, catching her outside the biology lab.

"Are you sure . . ." she began.

"Don't you want it?"

"Of course. But Ben gave it to you."

"And I'm giving it to you. For good luck."

"I know, but—"

Grace rounded on her. "Your brother's missing. You need good luck now."

"But you love him, too!" As she spoke, she couldn't help thinking of all the times Grace's attitude had puzzled and upset her.

Grace must have remembered also. She flushed and said, "I do love him! It's just . . ." Her voice wavered. She scurried into the lab.

At lunchtime Beth took refuge in the ladies' room. She stood uncertainly before the mirror. At last she clasped the necklace round her neck. Under the overhead light, the charm glinted like a shell through sunlit waters. Suddenly Beth was back on the beach at Cape Cod. Dave was with her. And Ben. She could hear them laughing. She bolted into a toilet cubicle. Hunched on the seat, she tried to cry. But no tears came.

Half an hour later she emerged still dry-eyed. Her chest felt squeezed; it was hard to breathe. As she went out into the hall she looked at her watch and exclaimed. One o'clock! She had missed lunch altogether. Not that she was hungry. But it was against school rules to cut.

Mr. Brown bore down on her. "No lunch, Beth?"

She would not answer. For once he seemed at a loss. "I . . . uh . . . can't tell you how sorry I . . . uh . . . we all are . . . about David."

She cut short the stumbling words. "I'm late for French." She felt his eyes on her as she walked away. She almost wished he would pursue her, offering an excuse to make a scene. But she reached her class unhindered.

Grace was in her seat already. Her eyes went straight to the necklace. She smiled. It made Beth uneasy. Impulsively she tore a scrap of paper from her notebook and scribbled, "I can't keep this. It would hurt Ben's feelings. See you after school." She undid the clasp and folded charm and chain into the note, passing it to her friend.

Grace took it, scowling. She read the note and, ignoring the French teacher's outrage, got up and walked over to hand it back. The gesture left no room for protest. Beth tucked the trinket away in her pocketbook again.

By day's end she was limp with pent-up emotion. Exhausted though she was, she hung around the lockers hoping Grace would come. She did not appear. At length Beth shrugged into her coat and trailed homeward.

As time went on, the sense of strangeness deepened. Dave seemed to have dropped right out of her life. Off the face of the earth, in fact. At intervals she would go to his door, as she had that far-off day when he left, repeating to herself, "Dave's gone. I may never see him again." The constriction in her chest grew. Still she could not cry.

She took to cutting lunch daily. She made no secret of it; instead hanging about the halls hoping someone would come after her. No one seemed to notice. Friends and teachers turned a blind eye. She supposed they meant it as a favor. It only increased her isolation.

She made several futile attempts to give back the charm. Grace would have none of it; she avoided Beth altogether. And despite her own distress, Beth could not help seeing something was terribly wrong with her friend. The ivory glow she envied had faded. Grace was a pasty white now, so drawn she looked scrawny. Her bones stuck out in ugly knobs. But it was her eyes that alarmed Beth. Beside the misery in them, her own pain was almost bearable. She ached for her friend. Even as she resented her. She was sick and tired of Grace's problems. It was her turn to be comforted!

By mid-December the weather turned bitter. Snow threatened daily from iron clouds. It only intensified Beth's dark mood. Even the Christmas displays failed to cheer her. They seemed forlorn and halfhearted.

The war news, too, had soured. On December sixteenth the Germans launched a last-ditch offensive through the Ardennes forest. Soon they had reoccupied great chunks of Belgium and Luxembourg. The 101st Airborne, besieged Bastogne, and General McAuliffe's defiant reply "Nuts!" to German demands for surrender, were on everyone's lips.

Beth overslept the Saturday before Christmas. When she woke at last she put on her bathrobe and crept downstairs, hoping for a leisurely breakfast with Jean and her father. But the house was silent and cold. A note on the kitchen table told her they were taking Grandma Michaels shopping and to lunch. They were making valiant efforts to distract the old woman, who had taken the uncertainty about Dave's fate hard. Still, Beth could not help feeling deserted.

She clattered about the kitchen making as much noise as she could to keep herself company. But in the end she plodded upstairs, leaving her breakfast untouched. The one good thing to come from the past weeks, she decided, was that she had lost weight. Her skirts hung loose.

The living room, as she passed, looked as uncared for as she felt. The glass from her father's nightly highball was still on the table. The ashtrays had not been emptied. She frowned. It was unlike Jean not to tidy up.

Something was missing, too. It took her a few minutes to identify it. Then it came to her. Christmas was only a few days off. But there were no decorations. No greens. No lights.

Galvanized, she ran upstairs to dress. She scrabbled through her piggy bank and produced a ten-dollar bill. More than enough for a tree. If she hurried, she could have it set up and decorated long before her family got home.

All the way to Third Avenue and back, she talked to Dave. "I'm doing this for you also. You'd help if you could. Remember when Jean and Dad both had flu at Christmas and we surprised them with a tree?" Passersby eyed her oddly; she went right on smiling and talking. Once she reached for Dave's hand and felt it close on hers, so vivid was his presence. She found it comforting.

She picked out a tree at one of the stands under the El. Spurning delivery, she dragged it home herself. She was hot and breathless by the time she got there. Leaning the bulky evergreen against the wall, she went to get the box of ornaments. Then she called Grace. It cost her a struggle. She longed to keep the surprise to herself. But she had promised Dave she would look after her.

Grace sounded so distant that all Beth's good intentions evaporated. She forced herself to say, "I just bought a Christmas tree. Want to come help decorate?"

"You're only just putting your tree up?"

"Dad and Jean didn't seem to feel like it. I thought it might cheer us up."

"Mummy had a decorator in to do ours. So it would be ready for her office cocktail party. It's very elegant. All white and gold. By the way," she went on with elaborate nonchalance, "Popsie's coming next week."

Beth tried to be pleased for her. All she could think of was the disastrous evening the year before. "Are you coming?" she repeated.

"I guess so. I have to bring your Christmas present. But I can't stay long."

Beth was just putting up the last string of lights when Grace arrived. She must have left in a hurry, because she was coatless and disheveled. Her hair was tousled, her skirt creased, and her cardigan buttoned awry.

"Aren't you frozen?" Beth blurted out. "You're mother'd kill you if she knew you went out like that."

"What do you mean?"

"Well, you know how fussy she is. And you don't have a coat on and—"

"So what?"

Aware she had been tactless, Beth backpedaled. "I guess it doesn't matter. Besides, they say it gets you used to cold."

"I told you," Grace snarled, "Mummy has nothing to do with

it. You either. Nobody tells me what to do or wear." She thrust a package at Beth. "Here's your present."

Beth loved gifts. But something in Grace's manner—furtive, even sly—gave her pause.

"Aren't you going to open it?"

Reluctantly she set the package on the piano bench and unwrapped it. Then she gasped. A dress was inside. The black silk rustled as she lifted it out; iridescent cross-bars gleamed.

"It's just like yours!" she exclaimed. "The one you wore last New Year's."

Grace giggled. "It is mine, silly. You liked it so much I decided to give it to you."

Beth recoiled. "I can't take it! What'll you wear for Ben?"

"Mummy will buy me another. Besides, I might not be here when he comes."

"What do you mean? Are you and Edith going on a trip?"

"Not Mummy. I might."

A shiver ran down Beth's spine. She whispered, "You're not going to run away, are you?"

Grace said nothing.

Beth was sorry she had spoken. She fell back on safer ground. "It's too small for me anyway."

"No, it's not. You've lost weight."

Baffled, Beth turned back to the tree and began to hang tinsel.

Grace said in a small voice, "I guess it wasn't such a great idea."

Beth swung about remorsefully. Grace sat in the Victorian chair. Meeting Beth's eye, she sneered, "You just love this stuff, don't you?"

"What stuff?"

Grace indicated the tree. "Christmas. I bet you still believe in Santa Claus."

Beth ignored the jibe. "Don't you like it?"

"I think it's infantile."

"You didn't used to feel like that. Remember when I spent Christmas with you in Philadelphia? And we made popcorn, and Ben helped trim the tree, and went caroling with us, and—"

"It was different then!" Grace cried in a strangled voice. She had gone so white Beth was afraid she would faint. Then in a bewildering mood shift, she rose and started for the door, saying calmly, "I have to go."

"Wait," Beth called after her. "What'll I do about the dress?"

"Keep it."

"Are you sure Edith won't mind?"

Grace smiled. "She'll never know the difference." The words were quiet, but face and voice alike chilled Beth. She did not hear the front door close. When she looked again, Grace was gone.

It was late afternoon when Robert and Jean got home. Grandma Michaels was with them. Beth braced herself for disapproval; to her delight her grandmother said, "Why, Beth! It's a lovely tree. Much nicer than the ones in department stores. You have a real flair."

Her father and Jean said little, but the look on their faces was enough. She hugged her father awkwardly.

"You put us to shame," he murmured. "Jean and I just hadn't the heart this year. We'll put up a menorah, too. Mother reminded us tonight is the first night of Hanukkah."

"Dave wouldn't want us to miss either," she said. "Not Hanukkah or Christmas." It was comforting to say her brother's name. It made him real again.

Despite her words, she dreaded Christmas. But there was a glow to it. A hard-won peace. She wasn't sure if it was the tree or the brave light of the Hanukkah candles on the mantel. For the first time in weeks she laughed out loud.

Jean had asked Julia and Tom to dinner. "This is no time to be apart," she declared. "Besides, it's hard on Beth splitting herself between two households."

They had after-dinner coffee before the fire in the living room. Robert Michaels was in a mellow mood. "That's a lovely dress, Beth," he said. "Is it new?"

She tensed. "Grace gave it to me."

Her mother must have seen her discomfort. She said quickly, "It's very becoming. You've lost weight, haven't you?"

Robert Michaels frowned. "It's a pretty expensive gift. I'm not sure—"

"She didn't buy it," Beth told him. "It was hers. She wore it last New Year's. Remember?"

Tom put his cup down. "Do you mean to say Grace gave you a dress of her own?"

"I tried to say no. She wouldn't let me." She thanked her lucky stars she hadn't worn the charm. What if they had seen and asked about it, too?

She glanced quickly at them, but they were not looking at her. Her father's face was shuttered. Tom and Julia stared at each other.

"What's wrong?" Beth said. "What did I do?"

"Nothing," said her mother. "It's not you. It's Grace."

"It doesn't sit right," Tom said.

"Can't friends give each other presents?"

He sighed. "Maybe we're making too much of it."

"I'll have a talk with Edith," Julia promised. "She should spend more time with Grace. Perhaps take a little vacation with her. She's so wrapped up in her own problems, she's forgotten the child. Now she's floundering. What do you think, Beth? How does she seem in school?"

All eyes were on her. She squirmed. Should she tell them of

Grace's anguish over Miss Gilles, the growing pile of undone assignments, the surliness, her threat to run away? But if she did, and her mother spoke of them to Edith . . . No! She could not do it. She would not betray a friend's trust.

"Let's not spoil the day talking about the Abbots," Jean implored.

Beth took a long breath. At least she wasn't the only one to feel that way.

Word came from the Red Cross two days before New Year's. Beth was out when the news came; she returned to find her father pacing the living room. His face was so wild she panicked, certain he would tell her Dave was dead. Instead, he hugged her so hard she yelped. He cried, "He's alive! He's a prisoner of war but he's alive."

When she disentangled herself, Beth said, "C'n I call Mom and Grace?"

"I've already spoken to Julia. But I know she'll want to talk to you. And you shall be the first to give Grace the good news."

An hour later she was talked out but happy. She had spoken to her mother and Tom. She had called the Siegels. They had been gratifyingly excited. Ruth Siegel had burst into tears and had to turn the phone over to her husband. Ruth had saved Grace for last. As she thought of the conversation, some of the shine was off the day. Grace had sounded quenched, as if joy were too much of an effort. In a drained voice, she had said, "Want to come spend the night? Mummy's going out. We'll have the place to ourselves."

Beth had acquiesced. More from shame that Grace knew how she felt about Edith, than any desire for her company. Especially in her present mood. Her father had been none too pleased to hear she was going. But Jean had said, "Let her go, Robert. We all agreed Grace needs extra attention. Meanwhile, you and I can go out to dinner and celebrate."

Beth was pleasantly surprised to find Grace in high spirits when she came. If she hadn't known better, she would have suspected her of sampling Edith's well-stocked bar. Her friend's cheeks were scarlet.

Grace dragged her out to the kitchen to show off a platter of sandwiches trimmed with parsley and dainty radish flowers, a bowl of hothouse grapes, and a luscious chocolate cake.

"Did you make all that yourself?"

Grace laughed. The old infectious gurgle Beth remembered. Her own spirits soared.

"Silly! I can't cook. I ordered from that fancy delicatessen on Lexington Avenue. Mummy won't mind. She left money for us to go out. I thought this would be more fun. A party. Like after graduation. Too bad it's too cold for the terrace. But we'll eat in the dining room and use the good china and silver."

Beth said nothing. She found the Abbots' dining room intimidating, with its mirrored walls and table that could easily seat twelve.

"After all," Grace said as they set the table, "it's not every day your best friend's brother comes back from the dead."

Beth giggled. Grace had pressed champagne on her and it had gone to her head. Giddily she raised her glass. "To Dave! My brother and your future husband. To all of us, in fact. You and Dave, and Ray and me. After the war's over, we'll live here in New York. And in a few years we'll get married and our kids can go to Jefferson. You'll be a great writer, and Ray will act, and Dave will be a lawyer like Dad, and I—" She stopped. Because she couldn't for the life of her think what she wanted to do when she grew up. She only knew she had to be with Ray. She brushed aside his vow to go to Palestine. He'd change his mind. She would see to it!

Grace smiled wryly. "To all of us. Wherever we land." She drained the glass.

"How can you drink so fast? It makes me dizzy."

"We have wine with dinner every night when Mummy's home."

Beth had a sudden picture of Grace and Edith eating supper every night in the huge cold room. Her basement kitchen, with its scarred linoleum and antiquated fixtures Jean complained of, was homey by comparison. Even her father's temper was preferable to Edith's icy fury.

"Don't you miss the old house sometimes?" she burst out. "And Ben?"

Grace's face went stony. "No. Popsie's not the same. Maybe he never was the way I thought. Most things aren't."

After supper they sprawled on the living room rug listening to records. Bach and Beethoven and Mozart. Popular favorites like "The White Cliffs of Dover" and "I'll Never Smile Again." The last never failed to bring a catch to Beth's throat.

It was midnight before they knew it. She yawned and stretched, saying sleepily, "Let's go to bed."

Grace did not answer. Glancing at her, Beth was shocked. Her face seemed shrunken, flesh stripped away to reveal the skull beneath. A death's head.

"What's wrong?"

Grace made an impatient gesture. "I'm tired. That's all. Come on. I have a surprise for you."

She pulled Beth along the hall, pausing at the door to her room to fumble for a key. Beth couldn't ever remember Grace locking it before. Then, as it opened, she stopped dead in her tracks.

The room looked as if a hurricane had struck. Clothes were everywhere—strewn on beds, chairs, bureau, and floor. All the books seemed to have been flung from the shelves.

"What happened?" she gasped.

Grace shrugged. "Just sorting out. I've got much too much stuff. So I'm giving it away." She scuttled across the room to gather up a pile and heap it into Beth's arms. "For you!" she announced.

"I can't take these!" Beth wailed. "I got in enough trouble over the dress."

Grace paid no attention. "Mummy's always buying me stuff I don't want. You might as well. I won't need 'em."

Beth said uneasily, "I thought you'd given up that idea."

"What idea?"

"Running away."

Grace stared. "Who said anything about running away?"

"You did. At least . . . I thought . . ."

The animation died from Grace's face. "Forget it. I'm tired. Let's go to bed."

Now Beth hesitated. "Shouldn't we clean up first?" It seemed vital to set the room to rights. To restore order.

"The maid comes tomorrow. She'll do it. Just shove those things off your bed."

Beth ached for home. But she could not abandon Grace amid the wreckage. She climbed into bed without washing and closed her eyes. She heard the light switch click; the room went dark. She lay waiting for the creak of Grace's bed. It did not come.

Opening her eyes, she sat up and looked around. The room was empty. She kicked off the covers and got up and went out into the hall. It was pitch-dark, but there was an icy draught around her ankles. Somewhere in the apartment, a window must be open. She groped her way to the living room. The terrace doors were ajar.

Beth went over and peered out. At first she could see nothing, but as her eyes grew accustomed to the gloom she made out Grace sitting on the glider.

"Grace?" she said uncertainly.

"What?"

"Come in. You'll get cold out there."

She came without protest. Beth closed and latched the doors and put her arm about her. She could hear her friend's teeth chattering. She hurried her back to bed and tucked her in. Like Mom, she thought with a pang.

By now her own feet were frozen. As she climbed under the covers, she heard Grace sigh.

"It'll be okay," she said. "Dave will come home safe."

"Get it through your head!" Grace cried. "I'm not going to marry Dave. I don't love him. I don't love anyone!" There was a desperate note to her voice.

"But you have to love someone. You can't live without loving."

Again Grace sighed. "It's no use. You don't understand." She was silent. Presently the sound of deep breathing told Beth that she slept.

Worn out with emotion, she dozed off soon after. She slept dreamlessly. Hours later she awoke to the glare of winter sunshine. She rolled over and rubbed her eyes. Then she looked at her watch. It was past nine.

Grace was nowhere to be seen. Beth got up and padded down the hall to Edith's room. It, too, was empty. She must long since have left for the office. There was no one in the kitchen; the debris of last night's feast was still on the table. Beth went back into the hall. Where could Grace be?

Just then she heard a faint rustling from the living room. "Grace?" she called. But when she went in, her friend was not there. The terrace doors swung open; the wind blew through them, riffling the pages of a magazine on the table.

Beth frowned. She could have sworn she had latched the

doors securely. She hesitated, then stepped outside, flinching as her bare feet touched the stone flags. The terrace, too, was empty, save for the shrouded forms of summer furniture. She could see the hollow in the glider cover where Grace had sat the night before. Somewhere in the street below a siren wailed.

The doorbell rang. Beth's heart leaped. Grace must have gone out and forgotten the key. She might at least have told me, she thought indignantly.

She scurried to the door. Words of welcome and reproach died on her lips. The elevator man stood there, a policeman at his shoulder.

"Is Mrs. Abbot in?" the policeman said.

"I think she went to the office."

"And you are . . . ?"

She did not want to answer. Something in his face compelled her. "I'm Beth Michaels. Grace's friend. I spent the night. They were both gone when I got up. I thought it was Grace at the door. . . ." Her voice trailed off. Then she whispered, "She's run away, hasn't she?"

"We'd better go inside," said the policeman. "I'll need Mrs. Abbot's office number. Is there someone you can call—your mother or father?"

Wordlessly she led them to the living room. She was ice-cold. Her knees were shaking so they would not hold her. She sank down on the sofa. She became aware the policeman was repeating, "Miss . . . miss . . ."

She searched their faces for reassurance. There was none there. Her lips were dry. She had to lick them before she spoke. "What is it?"

The policeman said again, "Is there someone you can call?"

"What's happened?"

"There's been an accident."

"Grace?"

He nodded. She saw the elevator man edge out onto the terrace and peer over the rail. There was something avid in the look. As if from far away, Beth heard Grace's voice that June evening, "Would you drift down like a feather? Or explode like a bomb?"

"I want my father!"

The policeman handed her the phone. As she dialed, she prayed, Let him be home. Please let him be home!

"Hello?" Robert Michaels said in her ear.

"Daddy?" She hadn't called him that in years.

"You'll have to talk louder. I can't hear you."

"Please come, Daddy."

"Beth! What's wrong?"

"I need you, Daddy. Come quickly!"

"Are you at Grace's?"

"Yes. Hurry, Daddy. Oh, hurry!"

The policeman took the receiver from her. "This is Officer Henderson, sir. There's been an accident. Yes, Grace Abbot. She fell or jumped from the terrace." Beth heard the exclamation from the other end. Then the policeman said reproachfully, "Oh, yes. She's dead. It's twenty-two floors down!"

17

Beth threw herself on her father when he came. He held her tightly, making no attempt to loosen the stranglehold. Presently he steered her toward the bedroom, murmuring, "Come, Bethie. You'll feel better when you're showered and dressed. The police will want to question you. And Edith will be here soon."

"I can't, Daddy!" she cried. "I can't see her. What will I say?"

"There's nothing to say. All we can do is be here for her."

"She'll ask why I didn't stop her. And I couldn't. I didn't know."

He laid his finger across her lips. "Hush, Bethie. How could you have known?"

"If only I hadn't slept late."

He gave her a gentle shake. "Now, pull yourself together. There's a good girl. Take a shower and put your clothes on. I'll wait in the living room. Try and be brave. The way you were while Dave was missing."

"Oh, Daddy!" she said, stricken. "I promised him I'd take care of her."

"You did. You were a good friend to her. Nobody could have done more."

But when they opened Grace's door, she saw naked shock on his face. "What happened? She was such a neat child."

"She tried to give me her clothes. I said I couldn't take them, but she wouldn't listen. Honest, Daddy."

He had gone white. Muttering, "It's stuffy in here," he threw open a window.

Without warning, the room seemed to tilt. Beth felt herself sliding—sliding helplessly downward. Twenty-two floors to the pavement below.

"Close it!" she screamed.

He was beside her in an instant, holding her till the dizziness passed. "It's all right, Bethie. I'm here. I won't let anything happen to you."

She managed a smile. "I'm okay now. I'll get dressed."

"That's my girl."

She stood under the shower until the hot torrents melted the ice encasing her. Then wrapping herself in a towel, she went back to the bedroom. She pulled on her clothes with shaking hands. Clothes she had chosen just the day before. It seemed a million years ago. She heard the front door slam. It was all she could do not to stuff her fingers in her ears. She did not want to hear Edith Abbot's voice. When she was ready, she forced herself out into the hall. At the door she turned and looked back. It was then she noticed the envelope propped against the mirror on the bureau. Her heart lurched.

Inside was a single sheet. "Dear Beth," it read. "I can't be what you and Dave want me to. I think I always knew that. But when you called to say he's safe, I was sure. Don't be too sad. You were right. No one can live without loving. But I can't love anyone. It hurts too much. I just want the pain to stop." There was no signature.

She did not know how long she stood there staring at the letter. At last she crept into the living room. To her dazed glance, it seemed teeming with people. The elevator man had gone but the policeman was still there, conferring with two men in business suits. She thought they must be detectives. Other people milled about. She recognized one of Edith's partners. He looked pale and shocked.

214

Edith was at the window gazing out; quiet as Beth was, she must have heard her come in. She whirled and rushed at her. Her eyes were terrible. Bright, and hot, and tearless. Beth shrank away.

Her father appeared from somewhere. He put his arm around her, steadying her.

"What happened last night?" Edith demanded. "You must tell me."

Beth swallowed. "Nothing. We had supper. She was happy about Dave. But later . . ." She gulped and started over. "Later, she said she didn't love him. She tried to give me her things. . . ." Her voice trailed off.

Edith's eye fell on the letter. Before Beth could protest, she snatched and read it. The silence was so intense it felt as though the world stopped breathing.

Edith shattered it. "God!"

Robert Michaels went to her, but she waved him away. She thrust the letter at Beth. "Take it. It's for you." Struggling to compose herself, she picked up the phone and began to dial.

"I'll make the calls for you," Robert Michaels protested.

She went right on as if she had not heard. Her voice was steady. "Operator? I want to place a long distance call. To the law offices of Abbot and Janeway in Los Angeles. Yes, I'll hold."

Someone touched Beth's shoulder. She turned to face one of the detectives.

"I'm Detective Donovan, miss. I'd like to take your story."

"Do I have to, Daddy?" she whispered.

"It will only take a few minutes," Robert Michaels told her.

"No one blames you," said the detective. "We're just trying to establish the facts."

"Are you taking me to the police station?"

"Of course not," said her father. "We'll sit over there in the corner where it's quiet. Don't be afraid. I'll be right beside you."

He pushed her into a chair and sat on the arm. The detective pulled up a chair facing them. He sat so close their knees almost touched. Haltingly Beth told of calling Grace the day before, and of her friend's invitation, of the disordered room, and Grace's pressing clothes on her. "I—I thought she was going to run away. If I'd known . . ."

The detective shook his head. "People sometimes give away possessions before attempting suicide." Seeing her face, he added quickly, "You couldn't have known that."

"But she was so happy at supper! She laughed the way she used to. It was like old times."

"Suicides are often happy just before the end. It's as if they're relieved to have come to a decision."

She went on to speak of finding Grace on the terrace and taking her back to bed, and of waking to the empty apartment that morning. At last in a voice so soft they could scarcely hear, she told of the arrival of the two men with the terrible news.

When she had finished the detective stuck his face in hers, forcing her to look at him. He spoke slowly and clearly as to a child. "I said it before and I'll say it again. Don't blame yourself. It wasn't your fault. You couldn't have known."

"But she gave me the charm. You know, Daddy. The one Ben gave her. And her black dress. If only—"

Her father interrupted. "None of us could have imagined." He turned almost angrily to the detective. "Can I take my daughter home now? This has been a terrible experience for her."

"Of course. But she'll have to leave the note with me." He held out his hand.

Beth's grip tightened on the letter. She would not give it up. She could not! It seemed the final treachery to reveal her friend's last words. The men were looking at her. Reluctantly she surrendered it.

"You'll get it back," said the detective. "As soon as I've finished my report."

Her father helped her to her feet. "Let's go home, love."

At that instant, the decorous hush of the room was shattered by sobs. All eyes turned to Edith. But she was still at the phone, receiver clamped between chin and shoulder, making notes on a legal pad.

Beth gritted her teeth. How could she sit there cool as a cucumber, when Grace . . .

Emma, the maid, broke free of the crowd and lumbered over to drop to her knees at Edith's side, embracing her and crying, "Oh, Mrs. Abbot! Oh, Mrs. Abbot." Tears blubbered her face.

Edith froze. Firmly she disengaged herself, distaste plain on her features.

Beth glanced at her father. His look was unreadable, but he was very white. He urged her into the foyer and helped her into her coat. She allowed him to button her into it. As he opened the door, she wailed, "My bag! I left it in Grace's room. I can't go back there."

"Jean's on her way. She'll bring it home."

"Shouldn't we say good-bye to Edith?"

"She's busy with arrangements." His tone chilled her. But she knew the anger was not for her.

Going down in the elevator, a thought struck her. She tugged at her father's sleeve. "Is—is she still out there? I don't want to see her that way."

His face softened. "It's all right. They've taken her away."

"Where?" She had to know.

"To the medical examiner's office. There will have to be an autopsy."

217

"They already know what happened!" An autopsy was like an operation. She could not bear to think of them cutting Grace up. Hadn't she been hurt enough?

"It's the law. Whenever there's an accidental death."

"Does—does Ben know?"

"He's on his way. He'll be here for the funeral."

Grace's funeral. She could not take it in.

She huddled against him on the cab seat, taking comfort in his closeness. To her dismay, he did not get out when they reached their house. "Aren't you coming in with me?"

"I have to go back to Edith's. Then to the office for a while."

Once inside she roamed restlessly, uncertain what to do or where to put herself. At last she crept into bed. But there was no refuge there. Grace's face lurked behind her closed lids, eyes full of wild entreaty. Over and over Beth saw her hurtle downward, heard her scream, and the thud of a body striking the pavement.

In desperation she got up and went to her jewelry box. She dug out the charm and stood clutching it; she could hear herself uttering hurt sounds like an injured puppy. She wiped her eyes and nose at last and stumbled downstairs to wait for her father and stepmother. It seemed a lifetime before they came home. Robert Michaels sagged into a chair. "God, I'm tired."

"Have you had anything to eat, Beth?" said Jean.

"I'm not hungry."

"It will make you feel better. Come on down to the kitchen. I'll throw some sandwiches together."

Sitting at the kitchen table, she could almost pretend it was a normal day. Almost but not quite. Try as she would, she could not hide from it. Grace Abbot was dead. She had killed herself.

"When's the funeral?" she said.

Her father's cup rattled against the saucer. "Next weekend

probably. When the medical examiner's report is in. And Ben gets here."

In school next week, Beth found that someone had already removed Grace's desk from homeroom. Rearranging the rows to hide the telltale gap. It made no difference. Grace's absence was more real than any presence. It drowned out everyone and everything. Like static. Beth thought surely others must hear it, too. But they went about their business seemingly oblivious. As they had when Dave was missing.

One night, she burst out, "How could she do this to me?"

"Do what?" her father said.

She was sorry she had spoken. The words sounded so selfish. "Kill herself," she whispered. "I told her everything would be okay."

Robert Michaels shook his head. "She didn't do it to you, Beth. It had nothing to do with you."

She managed to choke out, "She didn't even say good-bye!" and bolted before the tears spilled over.

Behind her, she heard her father say, "I don't mind telling you, Jean, everything—the refugees, the war, Dave, Grace's death—has gotten to me. I don't think I can take much more."

The day of the funeral was strangely springlike. The city basked under a pale sun; cirrus clouds laced the sky. As they walked toward the funeral parlor, Beth kept thinking, Oh, Grace! Why didn't you wait? Things would have worked out. And you'd have gotten over it. I know you would. I did!

The first person she saw inside was Ben. The old warmth was in his face, but she hung back. What'll I say to him, she wondered. What'll I do?

He bent to kiss her. Her nose wrinkled. He smelled stale like Grandma Michaels. She saw with shock that his hair was white.

Why, he's old, she thought. He's an old man. Torn between pity and distaste, she pulled away. She saw him wince.

Catching sight of Tom and her mother, she took refuge with them in the chapel. Flowers were everywhere—great bunches, and wreaths, and sprays. The fragrance was overpowering. An organ began to play "Jesu Joy of Man's Desiring." It had been Grace's favorite.

Her mother's hand touched hers; she didn't dare look at her. If she had she would have broken down. She tried desperately to think of something else. Anything to take her mind off what was happening. Try as she would, she could not shut out the coffin. Grace was inside. Her Grace. There but not there. Forever lost to her.

Ben stepped forward and began to speak. The words were no more than a jumble of sound; Beth understood nothing. In her confusion, she wondered if he would pledge that he and Edith would always be there for Grace. But that was what he had told her long ago. And he had been talking of Robert and Julia. Not Edith and himself. And whatever he might promise, he and Edith had not been there for Grace. Now Grace was dead.

Without warning, her stomach heaved. She blundered to the exit and stood outside in the mild air, gulping back nausea. Tom appeared. "You okay?"

She nodded. The turmoil in her stomach was subsiding.

"Have you eaten today?"

She shook her head. He took her arm and steered her down the street. From behind she heard the tap of heels, and turned to see Miss Gilles. "What are you doing here?" It came out as an accusation.

A wave of color stained the fine skin, but the teacher stood her ground. "I don't blame you for feeling that way."

"I have to go back, Tom," Beth said.

"The service is almost over. I told your parents we'd meet them at the Abbots' later. I want to get some food into you."

"What about . . . Grace?" she faltered.

"She's to be cremated. There's no burial."

They went into a Hamburger Heaven on Madison Avenue. Beth slid into a booth, trying to ignore the smell of frying meat. Was that how burning bodies smelled?

Again her stomach cramped. This time the gorge rose in her throat. She clapped her hands to her mouth.

"Quick!" said Miss Gilles. "I'll take you to the ladies' room."

They were just in time. The teacher held Beth's head as she retched. Afterward she wiped her face with a damp towel.

"Sorry," Beth muttered.

"Don't be. It's what I did when I heard. Only I didn't make the john. I had to use the office wastebasket."

"No. I meant I'm sorry I was rude."

Miss Gilles patted her cheek. "Your color's coming back. You were so white I thought you would faint."

Tom was waiting at the table. When he saw them, his face lit with relief. "Stupid of me not to think the smell might bother you. Shall we go somewhere else?"

"It's okay. I think I can eat something."

But she was still queasy. She ordered soup and ginger ale and sipped cautiously. Tom and Miss Gilles had hamburgers. Tom bit into his with gusto; juice spurted down his chin. Beth turned her eyes away. The teacher ate neatly but with dispatch. Beth thought they looked at once ravenous and guilty.

"You've nothing to reproach yourself with," said Miss Gilles. "The rest of us failed Grace. Not you. You couldn't have known."

"People keep saying that!" Beth cried. "But it's a lie. Grace told me she wouldn't be here when Ben came. I thought she

221

meant she was going to run away. I should have known better. If I'd said something, then maybe this wouldn't have happened. Maybe someone would have stopped her. But I didn't want to see or hear. I didn't want to think about it. I was sick and tired of her problems." She broke off, fighting for control. Then she heard herself say, "It wasn't Grace I worried about anyway. It was my mother. Last summer after you left, Tom, I was scared. Really scared. I thought Mom might . . . you know . . . do what Grace did." She fell silent, staring at the table. She went on more calmly, "Grace once said I don't like to talk about things that bother me. That I think they'll go away by themselves. Well, she was right. Only it's not just me. It's all of us. None of us wanted to see what was happening to Grace. And all the time she was . . ."

Tom reached for her hand. "Listen, Beth. It's too late for Grace. God knows, if I could change that I would. And maybe you're right. Maybe we were asleep at the switch. I don't know. But one thing I am sure of. I've seen your mother through some rough times. Like the divorce. Your father getting custody of you kids. I know Julia gets depressed. But she has real strength. She's a survivor."

Miss Gilles leaned forward. Her eyes behind the spectacles were intent. "As you yourself are, Beth."

"Why me and not Grace?" she whispered. "My parents got divorced, too."

"I wish I knew," Tom said. "All I'm sure of is that something went badly wrong for her. Perhaps it wasn't only the divorce. Perhaps Ben and Edith were blind to what she needed all along. Perhaps blindness is the one unforgivable sin. Not to see what's happening to people."

"But she and Ben were so good together!" Beth cried. "He was special. The perfect father. Oh, I don't understand. I don't understand anything!" She buried her face in her hands.

Tom said quickly, "Robert is special, too."

"Not like Ben. Dad's always angry. Always yelling."

"Has it ever occurred to you that he gets angry just because he sees things? Because he has the courage not to hide his eyes? Maybe he yells because he cares so much."

"But—"

"I know he has a temper," Tom went on. "But he has strength and integrity, too. More than most of us. Above all, he cares. He'd be a rich man if he didn't spend so much time helping people who can't afford to pay. Who do you think your mother runs to with her problems?"

"But I thought you and she—"

He gave a queer sound between a sigh and a groan. "Oh, I'm good company. But it's your father Julia leans on."

She couldn't help remembering his desertion after Grace's death. Again resentment flared. She was his daughter. Had Edith's need been greater than her own? Why did his family always come last? Yet he had come immediately when she called. And how safe she had felt in his arms. Was that how Grace had felt with Ben? If so, the loss when he went out of her life must have been unbearable. She could not bring herself to imagine it.

Dragging out the words, she said, "Sometimes I worry that Dad and Jean may split up, too."

"I hope not," Tom said. "For all your sakes. But if it happens, you'll survive that, too."

How did he know? How could he be so sure? Would she ever again be sure of anything?

"Have you heard from Ray?" said Miss Gilles.

"He's in Europe. He'll be all right." She said it to comfort herself. But the words rang true. Though she could not have explained the conviction. Ray would come back to her.

The teacher smiled. "A most talented young man. I expect to see his name in lights one day."

Beth shook her head. "He wants to go to Palestine."

"I'd go myself if I were younger," said Tom.

"You're not Jewish."

"We Irish have been fighting for independence long enough to sympathize. From what I hear, the Jews are doing exciting things there. Building a new society." He stubbed his cigarette out in the debris of the plate. Once the gesture would have disgusted Beth. She wondered how she could have failed to see his kindness and compassion.

Searching his pockets, he got to his feet. "I'll take care of the bill."

She watched apprehensively. Did he have any money? She could not bear to see him humiliated. She caught Miss Gilles's eye. The teacher smiled and put down a ten-dollar bill. "I always pay my way." Beth sighed with relief.

Out on the sidewalk an organ grinder cranked out tunes, a scrawny monkey at his side. The creature held up a cup as they passed. Beth leaned over to drop in a coin. Bony fingers gripped hers; she stared into a pair of bright hazel eyes. Beseeching eyes. Grace's eyes.

Sobs shook her. Rending tearing sobs. Tears streamed down her face. Tom pulled her against him. She stood gasping and shaking in his arms. Miss Gilles murmured soothingly.

At last she broke free. Tom gave her his handkerchief. "Better?"

She nodded, trying to suppress the gulps that racked her still.

"Best thing you could have done," he told her. "You can't bottle things up forever. That's what Julia does. I keep telling her, but she won't listen. Stubborn mother, stubborn daughter," he added with a smile.

"We should be at the Abbots' by now," Miss Gilles reminded them. "They'll be wondering where we are."

"Couldn't I go home?" Beth pleaded. "You could say I was sick."

"You have to face them sometime," said Tom.

"Not today."

"You know, Beth," Miss Gilles said, "soldiers who survive a war feel just the way you do. Both grateful and ashamed to be alive when others have died. There's a name for it. It's called survivors' guilt. You have to put it behind you."

Was that how her father felt about the Jews, she wondered. Was he ashamed to have been spared? In the same breath, she told herself she didn't care. What did it matter? No one knew or cared how she felt. Grace had been her friend. Not theirs.

Tom was staring at her; his look challenged.

"All right," she muttered. "I'll go. But I won't speak to Ben or Edith. Not ever again. I hate them!"

When they reached the Abbots', she stood rooted in the door. Unable to go forward or retreat. Tom had to propel her across the threshold. Inside, a kaleidoscope of faces, voices, smoke assailed her. Again she froze.

Then she saw her family. Edith sat on the couch, flanked by Robert and Julia. Momentarily Edith's face was unguarded; the despair there turned Beth cold. Robert Michaels must have seen, too. He put an arm about her. Julia bent toward her, talking quietly. Jean urged a cup of coffee on her. A faint smile curved Edith's lips.

Pride and love stirred in Beth. Whatever happened, they were there when they were needed. It was then she caught sight of Ben. He stood alone, staring blankly out across the room. All the fear and anger dropped away. She went to him unhesitatingly. Gently, so as not to startle him, she touched his sleeve. "Ben?"

For an instant she thought he did not know her. Then he smiled. She felt him quiver as she put her arms about him. A tearless tremor that shook his entire body. "I'm sorry, Ben," she whispered. "I'm so sorry!"

Over his shoulder, she met her father's eyes. Once again his lips framed the words, "That's my Bethie!"